DESERT FANGS

———•◈•———

James Johnson, illegitimate son of the legendary Wyatt Earp, moves his family to Texas to escape the perils of hero life. He makes a great deal on a homestead where the family can live an ordinary life. But the property was cheap for a reason.

Lurking in the shadows is a mythical monster. A creature built for killing with a taste for human flesh. The ordinary life James had bargained for is beginning to resemble his days in Dodge City. Fleeing his past might be impossible.

James, Sarah and Carson are about to find out why everything is BIG in Texas. And they must conquer the devil before it drags Texas down to Hell.

Will James return to his fighting ways? Can the family survive the beast's terror? Or will they be slaughtered one by one to feed the monster with their own blood?

Desert Fangs is the fourth novel in the *Son of Earp* series by Chuck Buda.

ALSO BY CHUCK BUDA

Gushers Series
The First Cut
Slashing Away
Tourniquet

The Debt Collector Series
Pay Up and Die
Delinquent
Bankrupt

Son of Earp Series
Curse of the Ancients
Haunted Gunslinger
Summoner of Souls

Visit my website to find all these books, and more!
www.authorchuckbuda.com

DESERT FANGS

CHUCK BUDA

This book is a work of fiction. Names, characters, places, and incidents either are the product of the author's imagination or are used fictitiously and any resemblance to actual persons, living or dead, business establishments, events, or locales is entirely coincidental.

DESERT FANGS
Copyright © 2020 by Chuck Buda
Edited by Jenny Adams
ISBN: 979-8663931410
www.authorchuckbuda.com

All rights reserved. No part of this book may be reproduced or transmitted in any form or by any means, electronic or mechanical, including photocopying, recording, or by any information storage and retrieval system, without permission in writing from the author, except by a reviewer who may quote brief passages in review.

Cover art © 2020 by Phil Yarnall | SMAYdesign.com
Interior design by Dullington Design Co.

The author greatly appreciates you taking the time to read his work. Please consider leaving a review wherever you bought this book or telling your friends or blog readers about this book to help spread the word.

Thank you for supporting my work. Without you the story would not be told.

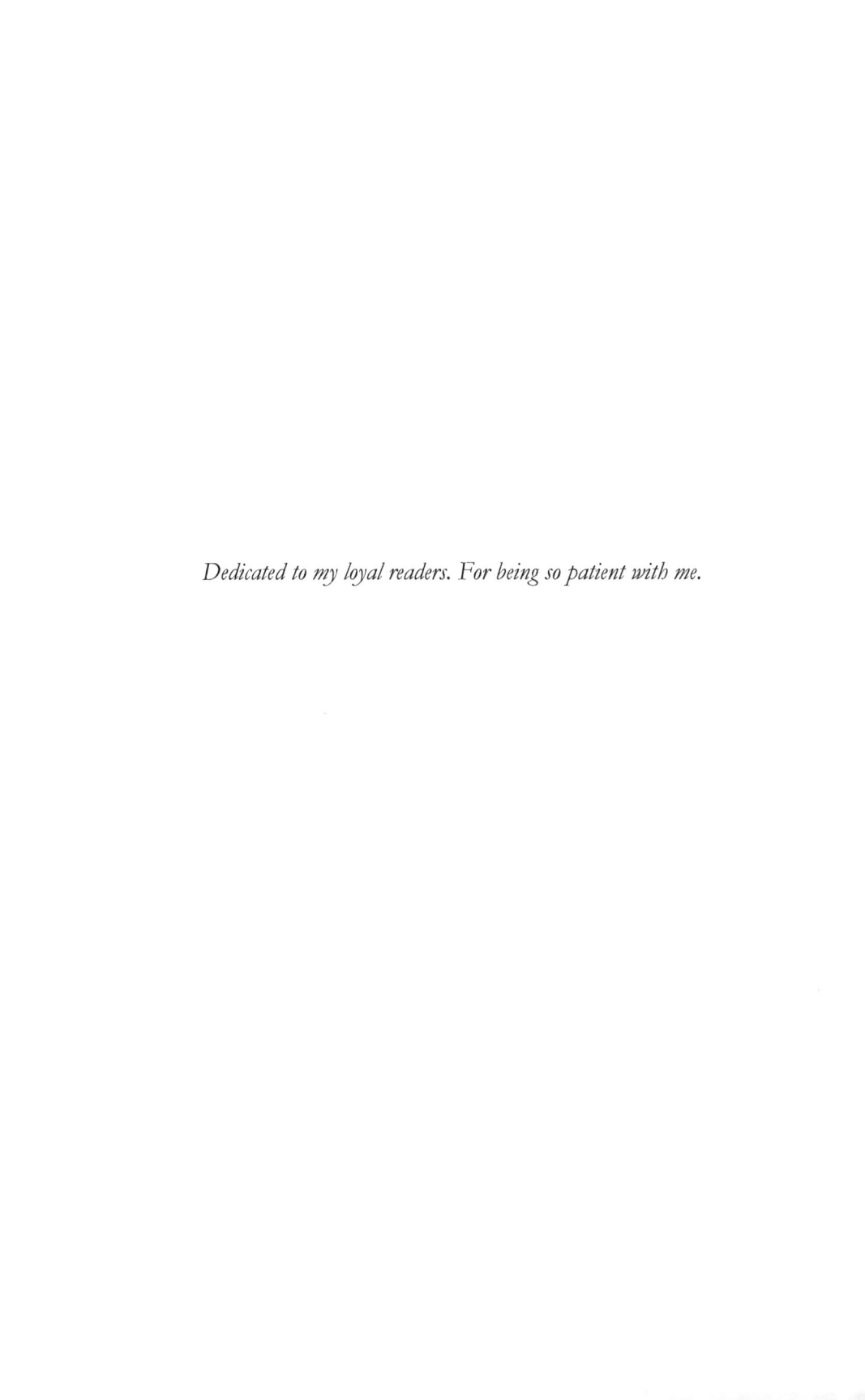

Dedicated to my loyal readers. For being so patient with me.

DESERT FANGS

CHAPTER 1

The arid temperatures in the vast plains of Texas provided little in the way of a substantive ecosystem. Most creatures, large and small, learned to move and feed under the cool blanket of nightfall. However, one species had chosen to do what was necessary to survive.

A true predator.

As darkness descended upon the land, a fearsome creature filled the shadows. It traveled beneath the range of hearing, hidden to the naked eye. A pack animal by nature, the alpha male ruled this region, almost unchallenged.

Only the settlers migrating west had been able to interrupt the reign of terror. Interruptions slowed the creature down and angered it.

Frothy saliva threatened to wet its paws before a tacky tongue retained what little moisture was available. Nostrils flared to breathe in the scent of fear. Tingles of excitement swam the fibers from the olfactory system to the predatory instincts hidden within the brain.

It was almost like a dinner bell.

A cornered whitetail deer, its back to an outcropping of rock, grunted and lowered its antlers to ward off the potential danger.

The beasts worked in unison, flanking the deer from multiple angles. A sly animal quietly sprang atop the outcropping. Fully surrounded, the whitetail snorted. It lifted its rack against the glow of the moon and bellowed a warning to its kin.

The alpha watched from outside the circle. Red, glowing orbs narrowed to scan the darkness for opponents. It knew the whitetail's cries would entice other predators to come in for an easy meal. Wolves and coyotes would quickly outnumber them. A mountain lion would put up a good fight, perhaps taking down one or two mates before giving up the battle. But the alpha wanted the nourishment. It needed it.

Meals had been growing scarcer. The opportunity within reach, the alpha growled, signaling the first wave.

First, a parry from the left. Before the snapping jaws backed away, another set of fangs drew near behind. Then another from the right. Each snip causing blood flow, but more importantly, stealing the will of the cornered animal to delay the inevitable.

The growl thundered louder.

The pack swarmed in. Bones splintered and flesh ripped. The whitetail attempted to dart through an apparent opening in the circle. It hobbled into the reach of the alpha.

His slavering maw snapped shut around the deer's furry throat. The fangs severed tissue and bone. The deer's head tore free from the neck in a bloody geyser. The horde pounced on the twitching remnants, a flurry of slurping and crunching as bones were torn apart. Mini battles flared over limbs and organ meat. Nothing was wasted in the fevered hunger.

The head of the deer rested at the feet of the alpha. He surveyed the destruction before him with pride. He would allow the pack to enjoy the spoils. For now. Then he would force them to hunt down the next meal. He knew hunting on a full belly was the smarter strategy. Waiting until the pangs of hunger roiled in their guts only increased their desperation. And disobedience. Their survival depended on his leadership. If the pack divided, they would be useless against the harsh realities of the desert. They would be as weak as the stubborn wolves and the back-biting coyotes.

He wouldn't have any of that.

The pack, still ravenous after leaving only clumps of fur and fragments of bone behind, licked their chops and stepped closer to the alpha. His red eyes widened toward the pack, warning them to leave the head for him. A few high-pitched whimpers drew his attention. They were still hungry and they sought an opportunity to move in on his serving.

The alpha knelt slowly, to show no fear amongst the tribe. He chewed off hunks of warm flesh and gnawed the ends of the spine. Salty marrow filled his mouth providing just enough flavor to dampen the taste of blood. As he ate, the alpha was careful to listen for the slightest bit of insurrection. His red orbs shielded behind their lids, taunted the others to think he wasn't paying attention to their desires. He dared them. Grunts and growls didn't deter his feast.

Before finishing the rest of the meat along the jaw and skull, the alpha rose, licking his lips and incisors to a fresh sheen. A pair of paws inched forward. The alpha lowered his head to clean the flesh between his claws. He sensed the daring of the younger pup so the alpha canted slightly away from the deer's head.

The opportunity was taken. A member of the pack lunged forward with selfishness. The alpha quickly set upon the beast. A new circle formed, barking and roaring from every angle, as the battle ensued. It was a quick fight and very one-sided. The one who dared to take more than its share ceased to breathe, its jugular torn wide in a fraction of a moment. The alpha snapped his jaws at the others, forcing them to backpedal lest they suffer a similar fate as their pack mate.

The alpha growled, a guttural grumble which crescendoed into an antagonistic warning. The crowd whimpered and disbursed outside the alpha's reach. He returned to the head of the fallen deer. Lifting his rear haunch, the alpha sprayed a pervasive stream of urine on the remnants of his meal. The message was clear. This meal is mine and nobody else's. He growled over his shoulder, leaving the deer head behind.

The pack shared hungry glances before descending on their fallen comrade. They ate heartily of their brother, fighting over the scraps and remains.

He hated the pack. Their existence was a product of his needs only. Strength in numbers. But he would just as soon feed on all of them and go on alone. The thought had surfaced periodically, a reminder that he was so much more than a mere pack animal. He was the ultimate killing machine and a follower of none.

Listening to the feeding behind him, the alpha leered at the half moon above. His thoughts turned toward their next meal. Survival was becoming more difficult as the moisture disappeared and the humans forced them away from the croplands. Eventually, the alpha would need to return to the croplands, where prey was abundant and water was rampant.

He would have to fight against the humans. There would be no other way to survive. They would have to make a stand or migrate further into desolate expanses of dirt and bramble. Their fate could no longer be avoided.

CHAPTER 2

James dabbed at the sweat dripping from his brow. Even though the morning was young, the dry heat of his new home in Texas began to climb. He dumped another bucket of slop for the pigs. The splatter painted the tips of his boots, adding texture to the dust and mud. He emptied the bucket with a few short jerks. Turning toward the wagon, James almost squashed a cheeky chicken as it scurried noisily under foot. James chuckled and shook his head.

Sarah waved at James across the yard. She paused momentarily to watch her son work the new farm. Well, the farm was new to them, but old in age, having been owned, for nearly a decade, by an old farmer and his family who had made their way west from Georgia. James waved back, resting the wooden bucket in the back of the wagon. He brushed off his hands on his pant legs, kicking dust devils as he went to his mother.

"Morning, James."

"Good morning. You're getting a jump on wash today?"

Sarah curled a wisp of dark hair behind her ear, her blue eyes soaking in the sunlight. "Well someone has to do it." She smiled at him.

James laughed. "I'd gladly switch jobs with you, if you'd rather get in there with Tina." He hooked a thumb at the over-sized hog and her brood. Sarah had chastised James for naming the huge mother after a human. She suggested something more in character, like Pinky or Snouty. Sarah thought it was disrespectful to women at large to have such a filthy beast named after one of their own. James had argued it was only a name, and nobody ever seemed to mind naming their horses or dogs after people.

Sarah rested her hands on her hips. "Did you hear the racket last night?"

James dusted his hat against a closed fist. "Yeah, it sure was loud." He squinted against the horizon as if searching for what might be out there, somewhere. "Guess it was quite a row between a few coyotes."

"I ain't never heard coyotes like that before." Sarah bent to pick up more laundry. She wrenched soapy water from a threadbare shirt. "The sounds were God-awful."

James nodded, staring at the tips of his boots. Rumors of devilish activity and strange disappearances of animals had probably figured into the good deal they had made when purchasing the farm. He had kept the stories a secret from his mother and Carson. James didn't want them to worry or be frightened about their new home. The price he had paid had afforded them the opportunity to start a new chapter together, far from all the horrors in Dodge City.

Only rumors, James reminded himself.

Rumors which happened to involve a person, too.

"I'm sure it was a territorial fight. A couple of coyotes getting into a row about a pretty young lady perhaps." James wiggled his eyebrows at his mother. She snorted with derision at his suggestion. "Carson must've slept through it all."

Sarah hung the shirt over a fraying string tied between the fence and a poplar tree. "He's usually under foot at this hour. Maybe the noise kept him awake. I'll check on him when I'm done."

James pivoted, there were more chores to do before breakfast. "We should keep it to ourselves. I don't want Carson to worry or be afraid. It's important that we get on here."

James had retired. That's what he had called it behind closed doors. His days of fighting evil and following in his Daddy's footsteps were over. James had decided to give up the life of adventure for a peaceful and safer existence, taking care of his mother and his best friend. He'd nearly lost them both. And Eleanor...

He yanked himself from the memories which plagued him at the oddest moments. James made his way back to the pens. The pigs had been fed but now he had to tend to the goats and the cow. He would have Carson sprinkle the leftovers for the chickens after breakfast.

The words of the townsfolk returned to James. Animals with throats torn apart. Missing pets and cattle. Like the night air had swallowed them whole without a trace of escape or foul play. And the person.

The former owner of the farm.

Gone.

Went to bed with his wife one evening. Heard a cacophony outside, grabbed his shotgun and went to take a look and never came back. Some say the farmer had had enough of his overbearing, overweight wife. Had decided to up and leave in the dark of night. Others whispered it was a far-fetched, unlikely scenario. More likely, the farmer had been whisked away by the same devils which had plagued the farm animals. Some sort of ghostly creature who carried away the farmer, into the underworld. Retribution for not going to church on Sundays like regular folk.

James didn't know who to believe. Partly, he didn't care to know. As long as he could afford the place and start a new life with his family. Away from the troubles of their past. A better life for Carson. The boy had been through enough already. And James wanted his mother to be happy. Safe. No more jobs whoring or being mistreated by priests.

Just a place they could call home. And live happily ever after.

James smiled to himself as he entered the goat pen. The kids nuzzled into his calves, excited to fill their bellies. Between the lack of rain and the endless nibbling of all the goats, the landscape inside the pen was mostly barren. James spoke gently to the smaller animals as they gathered around him. He stooped to hand feed some of the younger kids. He rubbed their frail necks and scratched behind their ears. Life was indeed good now. James was glad everything had fallen into place for them.

Last night concerned him.

James ignored the knot tightening in his gut. Something hadn't felt right about the disturbance last night. It sounded too...violent. They'd heard the wildlife active at night, but nothing like this. His thoughts turned to Carson. He wondered if Carson had been aware of the sounds or if he'd slept through it all. James hoped it was the latter. The noises had scared James half to death. He could only imagine what kind of impact they would have had on Carson, who was far more easily upset.

Carson's tougher than you think. Dang boy's been shot and beaten. He can handle more than others his age.

Maybe.

James cast his gaze towards the ranch. He'd hoped to catch Carson sprinting across the field with the excitement of a new day lifting his feet off the ground. Instead, the ranch looked quiet, like an empty picture frame with apparitions for eyes to replace the windows. James shivered. He hoped his instincts about last night were wrong.

For all their sakes.

CHAPTER 3

Carson was sleeping like the dead until James entered his bedroom to wake him up.

"Rise and shine, sleepy head."

Carson groaned. Typically, he sprang from bed each morning, ready to take on a new day of adventures and fun. But today Carson was tired. Very tired. The noises outside had kept him awake last night.

"You have to feed the chickens after breakfast." James picked up Carson's crumpled dungarees off the floor and tossed them onto the bed. It landed precariously over Carson's head. He quickly swatted the pants away from his face and shot James a glare. James giggled.

"I don't want to get up. I'm tired."

James glanced at the window. "Why are you tired? Did you stay up late counting cards again? I told you, you don't need any more practice. You're the best card player in the world." James scuffed a boot along the floor, accentuating his point.

Carson sat up, rubbing the crust from his eyelids. He yawned and tasted the thick film along his tongue. "I wasn't."

James ruffled Carson's hair. "Okay. Let's eat and then we can get to work."

Carson stared at James' back while he headed for the door.

"It was the Screeper."

James froze mid-step. He turned to face Carson with a quizzical expression.

"A what?"

"The Screeper."

"What in God's name is a screeper?" James glanced nervously at the window.

Carson pointed at the same window James had focused on. "The Screeper what made all the noise last night."

James sighed. He scratched at the persistent stubble along his jawline. "Only a couple coyotes scrapping over a woman."

Carson wrinkled his face. "What lady?"

James laughed hard. "Never mind. Get dressed and come down for breakfast. I'm making my famous dusty eggs." James shuffled out the door and down the hall.

As he sat on the edge of his bed, Carson thought about the sounds.

It was a monster.

Carson knew the sound of coyotes. What he had heard last night was no coyote. Not even a bunch of coyotes. The scary screams were like nothing he had ever heard before. It had sounded evil. Terrifying.

Hadn't James reacted funny too? He seemed as if he were hiding something from Carson. Like the way all adults lied to children when they wanted to pretend something was different than it really was. Like lying about his mother going off to visit relatives.

Like no monsters were outside the window.

Carson had bolted from his bed to the window when the first shrieks had sounded. He had clutched the window frame, peering cautiously over the ledge into the black void beyond. There had hardly been any moonlight due to the half-moon. He had strained his eyes in search of the creature that had made such horrific sounds.

Red dots.

Carson swore he had seen red dots far across the field. Or maybe he had only imagined it. Once he thought the red eyes had blinked, Carson jumped straight from the windowsill into his bed. He had scrunched his body into a ball and yanked the blanket over his head to hide from what he feared would come for him.

It had seen him watching. And it would want to get him now.

Carson had cried. Hard. He kept his sobs as quiet as he could so the monster wouldn't find him.

The Screeper.

He also didn't want James or Sarah to hear him. Carson worried they would come to his aid and the monster would dive through the window to eat them as they sat on the end of his bed to comfort him.

Whatever it was outside, Carson knew it was big. It had to be huge. The screams were too loud to come from a small animal. Growing up in nature, Carson knew what one coyote sounded like and he was familiar with a pack of coyotes. Their howls were distinctive; even in a pack, he could figure out the different beasts by their tones.

The Screeper.

Carson imagined the massive hunched shoulders of the monster he had heard last night. He gulped, choking on a pasty tongue. The thing had to have come from hell, the place he wasn't supposed to say out loud, but the preachers mentioned in their sermons. The sound of the devil.

He hurried to pull his dungarees on. Carson made sure to stand to the side of the window. He was afraid the Screeper watched him, even in the daylight. He wouldn't give the monster its chance to lunge through the window and gobble him up.

The smell of eggs cooking down the hall snapped Carson from his thoughts. He suddenly realized how hungry he was. And he loved James' dusty eggs. James liked to sprinkle an orange spice atop the scrambled eggs, some strange spice that Carson couldn't pronounce. He never remembered what it was called anyway. The first time James had slid the plate of spiced eggs in front of him, Carson had backed away, complaining that James had gotten his eggs dirty. He yelled at James for giving him dusty eggs and the name had stuck. James had forced Carson to try a bite and the taste was like magic in his mouth. Carson had gobbled up the spiced eggs and had asked for more. To this day, James' dusty eggs were a treat, a special breakfast for times when Carson wasn't feeling well or if they had wanted to celebrate some occasion like a birthday.

Carson wondered what was so special today. He shrugged to himself and flopped to the floor. Carson struggled to pull his boots on his feet. His boots were old and his feet had grown a bit. He kept forgetting to tell Sarah his boots didn't fit well anymore. He needed new footwear but Carson was afraid to ask because he knew how tight money was. He would try to ignore the aches and pain caused by the tightness. Maybe when he grew a beard like James, Sarah would take Carson into town to visit the cobbler for new boots. He smiled as he imagined the shiny, clean leather and the smell of new cowhide.

Carson stood. As he made his way to the door, he felt a creepy sensation fold over his shoulders. It came from the window. Carson hurried from his bedroom before the eyes behind him could catch up. He no longer wanted to spend any time in the first bedroom he had ever had to himself. He had been so happy to move into the room. Everything was his own.

Now it scared him to be alone.

CHAPTER 4

James nearly burned his hand. He had been so lost in his thoughts that he almost grabbed the pan handle without the rag. He understood the fear in Carson's eyes. His best friend had heard the terrifying sounds last night. And now he was afraid.

Sarah patted James' shoulder as she passed him. She began to place forks at the table and busied herself to pour water into three cups.

"I like the new James."

He rolled his eyes. His mother had made the same remark almost every day since they had settled at the ranch. It felt as if she wished to keep reminding James that he should do more cooking and cleaning and caring for the farm.

"I told you. I'm not new. I'm just a family man now."

Sarah chuckled. James flung a soggy piece of scrambled egg at her. It bounced off her apron and splatted on the floor. Sarah bent to clean up the mess.

James enjoyed the new life they had in Texas. Part of him missed the carefree timelessness of being a restless young man. But then, there was more routine in his day now. And it was much safer, which was by far the most important reason for his new lifestyle.

When it came to tools and farm work, James still felt out of sorts. It had only been a few months, and he continued to find himself in situations where he would waste time thinking about how to fix things. Or how to take care of the animals. Most of what James had learned, he had gleaned from listening to the townsfolk talk aloud about their own problems. Once or twice, James had mustered the courage to outright ask somebody for help on how to birth goats or clean chicken coops. And no matter how many times he measured wood before he cut it, the end result was always a whisker too long or too short.

"Did you wake Carson?"

"Yeah, he's getting dressed."

Sarah placed the pitcher of water in the center of the table. She laid out a couple of plates. "Any mention of the disturbance?"

James strained his ears to see if Carson was nearby. Feeling sure the boy was still in his room getting dressed, James responded over his shoulder. "He heard it. I think he's scared now."

Sarah cleared her throat, signaling Carson's arrival so James would cut the conversation short. "Good morning, Sunshine. Ready to get to work?"

Carson grumbled under his breath, making little eye contact as he squeezed into his seat at the table without pulling the chair back. James walked the pan over and began scooping dusty eggs onto the three plates. He made sure to serve his mother first. Then Carson. And whatever was left went on his own plate. He returned the pan to the counter.

James joined them at the table. Carson started to scoop eggs into his mouth when Sarah reminded him, they needed to say Grace first. Carson scrunched his brow with frustration. They held hands and repeated their practiced words, thanking God for the blessing of food and shelter and happiness together. They also mentioned all those loved ones who had passed on, including Carson's mother. James insisted they not utter Eleanor's name yet. He still found the wound too fresh and raw. She had been his first love and losing her so suddenly in Dodge City had been tough for him to accept. On the outside, James put on a show like he had moved on.

Inside his heart, a thick sadness remained.

Eleanor had helped James grow up, become more a man. Almost overnight, James had gone from dreaming about becoming his father to dreaming more about settling down. Finding a home. A place to call his own instead of bouncing from town to town. No longer having to live in cramped quarters above saloons. He had wanted to change for Eleanor. James wasn't interested in impressing her. He had wanted to provide for her.

The trio ate in silence for the entire meal. As the forks scraped along the plates for the last bites, Sarah broke the silence first.

"So, is today the day you are going to collect the eggs for us? Looks like we are about ready for some more." She leaned toward Carson as she spoke.

James slapped Carson's arm. "He's ready. Ain't you, buddy?"

Carson pursed his lips. James stifled a laugh. Carson looked so cute in his moodiness and with his greasy hair standing askew from a night of sleep. Carson protested that he was afraid of the birds. Sarah tried to convince Carson the birds were more afraid of him than he was of them. But James knew Carson hadn't forgotten the time a few chickens had pounced on him when he fell into the pile of feed. The chickens had dived in with reckless abandon, even as Carson kicked and cried in fear.

"James needs help. So do I. You're a big boy now. And what do big boys do?" Sarah tightened her bun, pulling the black hair. Her eyebrows raised, entreating Carson to respond.

Carson stared at his plate. He rested his head on his fist. "Help out."

"Contribute." Sarah reminded Carson.

James bit the inside of his cheek to keep from cracking up. Carson had difficulty pronouncing the word "contribute" so he had opted for the simpler "help out" after James had defined it for him. James wished Carson would go back to saying the bigger word.

"It's easy, buddy. You just go in, slide your hand underneath and take the egg. You put it in the basket and move to the next one. Simple." James acted out the instructions as he sat at the table.

"They bited me." Carson folded his arms across his chest and glowered underneath his grumpy brows.

"Chickens can't bite, sweety. They can only peck." Sarah used her hand to hide the growing smirk as she, like James, enjoyed Carson's stance. "Besides, they only pecked you because you were covered in feed and they were hungry."

James jumped in to try his hand at convincing Carson. "Or you can feed Tina and I'll do the chickens." James knew Carson was afraid of the big bruiser. He liked to throw the stale food items over the fence to the pigs rather than set foot inside the pen where Tina's girth would eclipse Carson.

Carson vehemently shook his head. "I'll learned the chickens."

James and Sarah both let go of their laughter. Carson's eyes accused each of them, darting back and forth.

James slapped the table. He loved Carson and enjoyed his little friend's quirks. James couldn't help but taunt Carson one more time.

"Back to square one."

Carson had had enough. He slid his chair away from the table as Sarah and James renewed a fit of laughter.

CHAPTER 5

The crisp night air brought a chill to Carson's arms. Dusk had shifted to darkness as they sat on the porch. Since they had moved, James had implored Carson and Sarah to sit with him each night before going to bed. The trio would watch the sun sink below the horizon and reminisce about the good times. Sometimes they would talk about their plans for the next day, covering the chores and assignments. Either way, James insisted they soak in the fresh air so they could get a good night's rest.

Carson hadn't adjusted yet to the extreme temperature changes in their new home. In Iowa and Kansas, if the day was warm then the night would be warm. If it had been cold during the day then the evening would be cold. But here in Texas, weather patterns were different. The days sweltered in heat, inhospitable to most living creatures, save the armadillos and rattlesnakes. Come nighttime, the temperature would drop to extreme lows, requiring afghans and jackets. James liked to sit in shirt sleeves because he said it cooled him off from all the hard work. Sarah would wrap herself in linens to keep the chill away. Carson usually wore his jacket, buttoned up to the place where the collar bit into his neck. Like his boots, Carson had recently outgrown some of his clothes as well. Tonight, he had joined James in shirt sleeves. As the goose flesh prickled his forearms, Carson pondered going inside for his coat. His legs were too tired to carry him though.

A strange whistle floated across the breeze. Carson stiffened as he instantly feared the Screeper was returning for his blood. He asked James if he had heard the whistle. James nodded and explained it away as the wind probably coursing through a hollow log or limb. Carson worried the monster was back, and nearer this time. James shook his head. He told Carson that sounds traveled farther in cooler weather than in the heat. He reasoned the sound could be coming from a mile away or so, and it only sounded like it was close. Sarah made no comments, which didn't ease Carson's fears.

He scanned the black ink across the yard for any sort of movement. Carson was sure the hulking chest of a wooly beast would emerge, saliva dripping from its fangs, just before it roared in their faces.

Sarah must've sensed his concerns. She scooted her chair closer to Carson, the legs screeching along the porch boards. Sarah stretched her arm around Carson's shoulder, tucking his head inside her afghan. He felt much safer inside her arms. The smell of outdoor air mixed with Sarah's lavender wash lulled Carson to sleep. His eyes drooped and his fears carried away with the wind. Carson drifted off as he listened to James and Sarah talk about their need for help. The farm had been much more work than they had anticipated. They needed the farm to survive. It provided shelter and food and a meager income. However, their labor wasn't enough to keep up with the workload required to sustain their lifestyle, much less grow it. James wanted to hire a hand from town to help out. Sarah chided James that they couldn't yet afford to take on someone's wages. She mentioned tightening their belts and saving some money in the bank first.

Carson's rhythmic breathing hid the anguish he felt in his slumber. He ran across the darkened field, tripping every few feet. The chickens pecked at his ankles, making him cry. But the chickens weren't his main concern. It was the Screeper. It followed him closely, chasing Carson back to the ranch. He could smell its foul breath and hear its bloody tongue slavering at its lips. The monster was hungry and Carson was the main course. He kept running. His lungs burned. It felt like his legs would just give up and collapse. They had carried him farther and faster than they ever had before. He stepped on a downed branch.

It snapped.

Carson sat up. His breathing came heavily as he stared into the darkness.

"What was that?"

Sarah rubbed Carson's back. "Just a twig, sweety."

Carson shot a look at James. He thought James concentrated all his energy on listening and looking too. The sound of the snapping branch was loud enough to wake Carson from his nightmare. It had also been loud enough to draw James' attention.

"It's time for bed now. Let's go to sleep. There'll be plenty to do tomorrow so we'll need all the rest we can get." Sarah lifted Carson so she could stand. She pulled the afghan tight around her torso and made her way to the door.

"I'm ascared." Carson hyperventilated. He knew the Screeper would visit his window tonight.

James rose from his chair. He stretched his arms high above his head and then twisted to the right, his spine cracking with the motion. "Nothing to be scared of, Carson. It's just a branch or something. Lots of noises at night. You know that."

Carson stared into the black. He scrambled behind his chair and peeked over the high back. James neared him. He squatted down and whispered into Carson's ear.

"Remember when we used to sleep under the tree roots in Iowa? We'd always hear things scrounging for food or howling at the moon. We weren't scared back then, right?"

Carson remembered. He wondered if they were just foolish all that time ago or if they had lived in a place where there weren't any monsters. This place was different. It felt different. Carson never felt completely settled in Texas.

"But...here there's a Screeper."

James patted Carson's shoulder. He let out a long breath. "Well, I don't think there's no such thing called a Screeper." He stood up and tugged at Carson's elbow. "But I'll tell you what. What do you say that we camp out tonight? Like the old days?"

"Uh-uh. I ain't sleeping out here."

James chuckled. "I mean we will pretend to camp out. I'll grab my pillow and I'll come sleep in your room. On the floor. Just like we used to do in our hidden fort. What do you think?"

Carson smiled. The thought of James staying with him shooed away all his fears. He would get some sleep while James looked out for him. Carson was pleased since he wouldn't have to run into James' or Sarah's bedrooms in the middle of night, screaming with terror.

Carson hoped James would sleep with him every night, and not just this one time. Especially since Carson knew the Screeper really did exist. And it waited for him out there.

Somewhere.

CHAPTER 6

Carson aimed the gun. He pulled the trigger, hearing the imaginary report of the gunshot. The wooden replica felt heavy in his small hand. He secretly wished he could have a toy gun instead of pretending with his finger and thumb. In Dodge City, Carson had found a stick which was shaped like a revolver. The best part was the size; it fit perfectly like a gun made just for his hand. Carson wished he had remembered to retrieve it from the yard before they had set out for Texas.

He placed the toy gun back on the shelf. Sarah had tasked him with very specific items to buy. She needed Carson to pick up a few things while she attended to their account at the bank. Then she had to inquire about some potential work at the dressmaker's shop. On the ride into town, Sarah had explained how she had come up with an idea to do some stitching and needlework. If she could make a few extra dollars each month, they could afford to hire some help for the farm. She hoped they would accept her offer to do some sewing either a few days per week, or, preferably, allow her to do the stitching at the ranch. Sarah would bring the finished products to town, get paid, and then return to the farm to split duties between ranch work and stitching.

Carson jammed his tongue into the side of his mouth, trying to recall what Sarah had asked him to buy. She needed soap and...something else. He touched some of the products sitting on the shelves as he scanned the inventory, hoping to see what else Sarah wanted. Maybe the item would jog his memory.

As he lingered down the aisle, Carson realized somebody on the opposite side of the shelf spoke in an excited tone. Carson leaned into the shelf, poking his face between a few bags so he could see the speakers.

An older gentleman with a crushed hat and unkempt mustache became animated as he used his hands to accentuate his story. The other man, wearing a top hat and coat tails, stood with his arms crossed. Carson got the impression the well-dressed gentleman found the other man's tale to be unbelievable.

"Like I told you before, ain't no bears in these parts. What I seen was like nothing I seen before."

"Gowdy, I am an educated man and I refuse to hear of such nonsense. The thing you described can only be a bear. Maybe it wandered this way or got lost."

"Bears don't make sounds like he done." Gowdy held his hands to his ears as if the noise scared him again.

Carson swallowed a lump and leaned closer. He wanted to know if Gowdy had seen the Screeper. His knees felt shaky as he used the shelf to hold himself steady.

"And bears don't destroy their meat. Not like this. There was flesh everywhere. The blood was all gone. Sucked clean out. I never seen a carcass in all my days looked nothing like that. It was monstrous." Gowdy poked a finger into the gentleman's chest to drive home his last point.

Carson slipped off the shelf. His hand knocked over a can of beans. The gentleman shot Carson a look through the shelving. Carson scrambled to the floor to pick up the can he had knocked over. He stretched his arm over his head to place the can back in its place without standing. He didn't want the man to see him again. He was afraid the man would holler at him for listening in where he didn't belong. Carson crawled a few feet to the left. He raised on his knees. It stared him in the face. The box of soap flakes. Carson snatched the box, remembering he had to get the items and meet up with Sarah at the wagon outside.

He strained his ears to continue eavesdropping. Gowdy went on to reveal explicit details about the horrific scene, and its personal effects on his digestive system. Gowdy told how he felt as if he were being watched and he feared for his own life. He likened the event to similar occurrences around town. So and so's dog. This one's prize steer. That one's work horse. Gowdy brought up the sounds he kept hearing at night. He imitated the same shrieks Carson had heard back at the ranch. His blood froze in his veins. He suddenly realized how hard his hands gripped the box of soap as both corners crumbled inward. Gowdy released another awful shrieking imitation. It upset Carson to the point where he had to get out of the store as quickly as possible. The screams were too close to the real thing. Carson felt he would empty his bladder in his pants.

As Carson hurried down the aisle toward the front door, he knew he would get yelled at for not doing his part to help Sarah. But he couldn't help himself. Carson had never felt terror like this in his life. The Screeper was a real monster. And whether anyone believed him or the man Gowdy or not, that thing was as real as a pile of horse dung in the street.

Carson rounded the end of the aisle. He slammed into a tower of a man. His chin smashed into a tarnished belt buckle, opening a small slit of a wound under his lips. Before Carson could scream out in shock, he was spun around and lifted off the floor by the back of his shirt collar. The man's hands felt stronger than an iron rail and bigger than a box car. The smell of unwashed sweat permeated Carson's nostrils, sucking the air from his lungs. He kicked his feet back and forth like he could run across the clouds. His hands held tight to the box of soap flakes. As much as he felt he could use the box to fend off the gigantic kidnapper, Carson wanted to show Sarah he had at least remembered to get one of the items on her list.

The man carried the boy to the front of the store, where the proprietor stood behind the counter with a surprised expression on his bearded face. He kept his pencil poised above a small note pad. Carson was disappointed the proprietor did nothing to help save him from the large man.

"Put it on my account." The gruff voice scared Carson almost as much as the sounds of the Screeper. His bladder no longer retained its contents.

CHAPTER 7

Sarah crossed the street with an extra hop in her step. She wanted to bound across the bustling road, feeling as if she could float upon a fluffy cloud. Her meeting with the dressmaker had gone better than expected. Sarah had been nervous about inquiring to become a commissioned stitcher but she had forced herself to pitch her idea anyway. She recalled something her mother used to tell her when she was a young girl. WHAT'S THE WORST THEY CAN SAY? NO. Sarah knew in her heart that her mother's sage advice had always proved true. Yet, Sarah felt there was so much more riding on the question this time.

She carefully lifted up her skirt to avoid brushing the fresh horse droppings. With her arms full of fabrics, she nearly lost her balance trying to do too much at once. Images of poop-stained fabrics and losing her new job brought butterflies to her belly. Sarah regained her balance and hurried along to the wagon she had left outside the general store. She was surprised that Carson wasn't waiting for her in the wagon. She snickered to herself how she would have to go inside to help him complete his task. Sarah knew he sometimes struggled with the things she asked of him but she hoped treating him like an ordinary boy would help Carson grow stronger, able to live more independently.

As she flopped the fabrics over the back of the wagon, the sound of the store's door slamming shut caught Sarah's attention. She looked up to find Carson dangling in midair.

A very large man stood along the edge of the raised porch. His strength was evident as he held Carson aloft with one hand. Sarah wondered how the collar of Carson's shirt held up to his weight dangling off the ground. Carson's feet kicked around like he was running across an amber field of grains.

"This belong to you?"

Sarah stared up at the burly man. His thick beard draped over the chest of his shirt. The man's hat dipped low, shielding his eyes and most of his face from being seen. Sarah immediately worried what she would have to pay in order to clean up whatever mess Carson had caused. She imagined him accidentally knocking over a large display of glass medicine bottles or something else expensive.

"Yes. He's my son. What happened?"

The man spat a huge wad of brown juice which splashed the planks at his feet. "Caught him stealing. He'll have to go to jail now for breaking the law."

Sarah wrung her hands. Her fears of owing money she didn't have were replaced with worries of how to get Carson out of jail. Dealing with the law would be much more difficult than promissory notes or free labor to pay off debts.

"Oh, please don't take him away, sir. He's..." Sarah tried to dance around the fact that Carson was special. She didn't want to hurt Carson's feelings but she needed to convey his special situation in order to get him out of trouble. "He's not like other boys. I'm sure he didn't understand what he was doing."

The man pointed at the box of soap in Carson's hand. He held Carson further over the edge of the raised porch. "If he ain't know what he done, then why is he still holding the box of suds?"

Sarah glanced at the box of soap which had been squeezed into a less square shape in Carson's grip. "Oh, see, that was my fault. I told him to pick up some items for me while I was attending to other business. I gave him some money to pay for it." Sarah turned her attention to Carson. "Show him the money, sweetie."

Carson's legs began kicking harder. He grunted as he tried to escape the large man's grasp. His struggles were to no avail as the large man tucked Carson under his arm as effortlessly as if he were a satchel of deeds.

"So you put him up to stealing, is that it?"

Sarah waved her hands, exasperated with the turn of events. If she wasn't careful, they'd both end up in jail and James wouldn't know what had happened to them.

"No. No, that's not what I meant. I gave him money to buy the things we needed and then we were going to head back to the farm. Please. I think there has been a big misunderstanding. Can I just empty his pockets to give you the money for the soap? We don't want any trouble."

Sarah tinkered with the notion of turning on the water works. She had found that even the biggest, scariest men softened when a pretty woman cried. She remembered another one of her mother's pieces of wisdom from her childhood. WHEN YOU DON'T HAVE MUSIC TO SOOTHE THE SAVAGE BEAST, USE YOUR TEARS. The sage advice had saved her on several occasions when she was a whore.

The large man dropped Carson to his feet. Carson scrambled down the stairs and climbed into the back of the wagon. He ducked under the rolls of fabric to hide from his captor.

"I guess we can come to some kind of arrangement."

Sarah's stomach sank. She understood what the word 'arrangement' meant whenever she dealt with dirty men. It would mean she would have to degrade herself for his pleasure in order to make amends. Sarah was no stranger to the unwritten customs of the West.

Before she could answer the man with her alternatives to his suggestion, he lifted the brim of his hat and stared directly into Sarah's eyes. She recognized familiarity behind the dark irises and the worn laugh lines, but she couldn't immediately place the man's face. As the stranger smiled, Sarah's heart skipped a beat. She realized who the man was and her surprise at finding him here was quickly overwhelmed with her desire to run and jump into his muscular arms.

"George!"

Sarah held her hands to her mouth in disbelief. George removed his hat and ran a large hand through the long dark hair that hung close to his face. He nodded his acknowledgement to Sarah's recognition.

"My goodness. It's been so long. I can't believe we've run into each other again. What on earth brought you here?"

George looked nervously at his dusty boots. He glanced up the street and then returned his attention to Sarah.

"You. I came looking for you, Sarah."

CHAPTER 8

The dry heat had already begun to sap James of his energy. And it wasn't even noon yet. James could tell his horse felt the same way. It paused every so often, slowing the action of the plow. It was aggravating James because it required more energy from both of them to re-start the plow after its momentum came to a halt.

He used his sleeve to dab away the sweat that dripped from his brow. James cursed under his breath, chastising himself for leaving the bandana on the porch rail. He had meant to scoop it up on his way to the fields but he had been distracted by the animals.

The pen of creatures had erupted with unease, bellowing and trotting away as if they had been chased by an unseen predator. James laughed it off before remembering the sounds they had heard the other night. Even Carson had sensed the dread of something lurking in the shadows. An animal unfamiliar to them.

James forced the horse to lunge forward with a sharp whistle and slap to its rump. The horse whined and lurched ahead, hefting the weight of the plow as it dug into the arid soil. James exhaled with relief at not having to use more persuasive actions with the horse.

As they covered several more swaths of land, James was torn from his focus by another outburst. The goats and pigs had nearly trampled each other as they ran for the far side of the pen. The chickens flapped and flitted in chaotic motion, dancing around nervously. James cursed aloud and yanked the reigns to stop the horse. He rubbed its nose and offered it a "Good girl" followed by a couple of clicks of his tongue to order her to stay in place. The horse huffed and lowered its nose to the ground.

James removed his hat, fanning his sweaty head as he hurried to the pen. The hairs along the back of his neck stood on end. He stopped in place, straining to hear anything that might signal him as to where the creepy feeling had come from. His eyes darted along the farm, scanning the wood line for any movement.

Or eyes.

The animals settled and returned to their normal behavior. Tina came running for James as if her dinner bell had rung once again. She sniffed at James' boots, nudging his legs with her filthy snout. James rubbed Tina behind her ears and brushed past her to the west side of the fence line. All the animals had headed east, in the opposite direction, to escape whatever danger they had sensed.

James bent to inspect the fence line. The dirt had been disturbed in several places. Clear signs of coyotes attempting to breach the pen in order to hit pay dirt. It would be an endless buffet if they could make it inside. James wondered if they would start with the low-hanging fruit of the chickens or go right for the jugular, taking down Tina and some of the larger "meals" in order to make the most of their strike.

He rose to his feet, brushing the dirt from his hands along his pants. His eyes returned to the wood line. His instincts told him that would be the most likely hiding spot for a predator. The land was mostly flat, with only a few hills to break the horizon. But the wooded outcropping created a natural wall that hid the game trail that meandered toward the river. It stretched for miles along a rocky expanse.

James scratched his head. He'd need to set a trap along the wood line, something to snare whatever had been hunting his animals. Coyotes traveled in packs. He'd have to devise a plan to snatch them all at once or grab as many as he could at one time. Hopefully, it would deter the rest of the pack and they would move on.

And if it's not coyotes?

James shuddered. His gut told him he was up against something much more dangerous than a pack of dogs. The sounds they had heard. Like nothing they had experienced before. It worried him, imagining what kind of creature could be circling the farm. The rumors of the farmer's disappearance. His family's desire to sell the farm for a pittance and clear out of Texas as fast as they could.

It had all been so strange. He wondered if he should have paid more attention to the warnings. To the rumors. James had been too motivated to take advantage of the opportunity. The fresh start. The safety and comfort of leading a simpler life.

James crossed the field to get back to work. The horse had stayed in place, grazing on what little scraps of growth tufted the surface of the dry earth. James stumbled as his boot caught in a divot. He hit the ground hard, sending up a plume of dust swirling around his head. He collected himself, torn between cursing his luck and laughing at his clumsiness. James put his hat back on his head and scuffed his boot along the dirt as if he were punishing the ground for tripping him up.

He squinted and then his eyes opened wide.

James bent to see the hole which had caused his fall. The spot had not been an ordinary rabbit hole. Nor had it been a crater from moving a large rock out of place.

It was a paw print.

James ran his finger along the outside of the mark. Whatever had left the print had been heavy enough to push the earth down a quarter inch. And in such dry conditions, James knew that was no small feat. He understood the beast had to be big. The size of the print further corroborated his notion. It would take several coyote paws to fill this one track. There'd be no way a coyote could leave such a print. A wolf? James considered the idea but wolves tended to live up north where the land was more hospitable to their large bodies and heavy fur. The possibility did exist, as unlikely as it was.

James needed a bigger trap.

He spent several minutes tracing the print, comparing it to the size of his own boot. The day's work threatened to go undone so James pushed himself to return to the plow. The work time would provide him ample opportunity to contemplate his next move and the design of a trap strong enough to harness whatever animal came sniffing around his farm, too close for comfort.

CHAPTER 9

The azure sky stretched into oblivion, dotted with wisps of cirrus clouds. As the afternoon sun began to shift across the landscape, James took a break from the chores to check on the traps he had been setting each day.

James whistled with glee as he walked up on the trap line. He clapped his hands with pride. Maybe he had finally gotten the hang of trapping in these parts. The family would get some much-needed protein in their dinner tonight. The very first trap bore fruit. A lean rabbit wriggled in the snare. Its slow-motion struggles hinted at the animal's near demise. James snatched a sizable rock and quickly dispatched the rabbit to end its misery. He loosened the snare and carried the rabbit by its rear haunches on his way to inspect the rest of the trap line. He had caught two ground squirrels as well. James hooted to the wide-open expanse and did his best to celebrate his booty with a two-step shuffle, kicking up dust clouds. The animals were small but he'd be able to provide a few ounces of meat for each of them.

He hurried back to the ranch so he could clean the animals before they soured in the Texas heat. James laid them out along the chopping block and pulled his knife from its sheath. He noticed the blade had dulled since they had arrived at the homestead; now that he had become a working man, James had put the blade to use on a daily basis, giving the knife a practical purpose rather than existing for show like it had in the past. He started to work on the rabbit, slicing from the back of the skull along the spine until he reached the rump. James peeled the pelt down around each limb until it tore free from the flesh. Small clumps of fur lifted into the air as if escaping from the shiny blade. James didn't mind cleaning game animals but it was still his least favorite chore. He smirked at the memory of his first cleaning. James had caught a field mouse, tiny and frail. He had marveled at how light it was. The small leg bones had felt like weak branches on a dead tree. James had lost his breakfast, mostly on the tips of his boots, when he had attempted to gut the creature. He had ruptured the bladder and large intestine, releasing the noxious scent of inner workings and waste materials. It had never dawned on him that the insides of living things could smell bad. James had figured the smelly stuff came out when using the outhouse. The realization that the gut still harbored putrid odors had brought about another round of vomiting. James snickered to himself as his mind walked through the past. He finished freeing the pelt and re-positioned the rabbit so he could cut off the rear legs.

Tina snorted, drawing James' attention away. He glanced at the pen as Tina nuzzled the smaller hogs way from her corner. She had worked the slop on her side of the pen and had decided not to share it with the smaller pigs. In the background, James picked out movement along the horizon.

A wagon rolled along the trail toward the farm. A long dusty cloud billowed behind it, frothy and smoky nearest the wagon, and ghostly as it dissipated into the heat further back. James waved at them even though he knew they were too far away to see his arm. The excitement of sharing his catch swelled to bursting in his skin. He couldn't wait to show his mother the fruits of his labor. She would be happy to cook something with more flavor. And he hoped she would be proud of the job he had been doing as he developed into the family man he had promised her.

Carson might be a different story. Carson loved to hunt and track animals. He enjoyed eating the meat too. But Carson still squirmed at guts and blood, especially from animals. It wouldn't bother Carson to see a cut on James' hand or even a gash on his own body, like the time

Carson had been shot. However, something about the small, cuddly animals always set Carson into fits of disgust or sadness.

James waved again, unable to contain his enthusiasm. As the wagon drew nearer, James began to lose his smile. His brow furrowed as he squinted.

They weren't alone.

His mother and Carson rode in the wagon. But a few paces behind them followed a lone horseman. A pang of worry roiled in his belly. Were they being chased from town? Followed by a highwayman? Had something gone wrong while they were in town? Or maybe his mother had decided to hire help for the farm. The last notion didn't sit well with James because he knew how responsible his mother was. She wouldn't commit to owing someone else money without having funds set aside for such a prospect. And they weren't quite there yet with their meager savings.

It had to be trouble then.

James stuck the knife in the stump and brushed his bloody hands in the dirt to clean them off. He began to back toward the house in an instinctual protective posture. The wagon rounded the slight bend in the trail, heading directly toward him. As it grew closer, James could see the expressions on their faces. They appeared happy. Not distressed.

And James saw the lone rider.

His emotions bounced between disbelief and happiness. He realized who had joined his mother and Carson.

George.

James tried to figure out how his old friend had crossed paths with them. Texas was a long way from Iowa. And James had never thought he would ever see George again.

Yet, here he was. In Texas.

James waved at them again as they rolled up to the ranch. Whatever pride and excitement he had about his trap line yield had quickly been replaced by wonder at the prospects of their new visitor. And old friend.

He ran to meet them as they pulled to a stop. Carson bounded down from the wagon. He pointed back to George and shouted.

"George getted me out of jail."

Carson squeezed James in a choking hug.

James couldn't wait to hear the story of their trip to town.

CHAPTER 10

The reunion had been a blessing. Sarah was glad to see George again. It was comforting to have a familiar face around their new environment. If George would be willing to stick around, his help on the farm would be a welcome addition. George's skills with fighting and shooting would also ease the fear they had about what might be lurking on the outskirts of their land.

Sarah blushed as she recalled George's admission that he had been looking for her. She'd never had feelings for George beyond a working relationship and a mild friendship. But somehow his reappearance had triggered something deep within her. The way he had said it.

"You. I came looking for you, Sarah."

James had been shocked to see George. They had quickly picked up where they'd left off after bonding in the hunt for Crouching Bear. James had shown off what he had caught in his traps. George mocked him for only being able to kill small animals. He had joked that they were good catches for a kid, but he would need to work up to more manly-sized animals. James, reddened with frustration, started to argue his side until he realized George was only kidding him. They washed up and talked at the table while Sarah cooked the meat.

They laughed at George's story of how he had scared Carson in the general store. He had been picking up supplies when he recognized Carson rummaging through the shelves. Carson had been running through the store and George had taken the opportunity to surprise the boy. He had figured Carson would lead him to James, but he'd been happy to find Sarah instead.

"So, what brought you to Texas?"

"I'd grown tired of Pella. Thought maybe I'd hit the road in search of adventure." George leaned back in his chair.

"Of all the places in the world. It's funny we'd run into each other in Texas." James helped Carson set the table, placing forks and knives at each seat.

George tapped his long fingers on the table. "Well, I was counting on crossing paths with you again. Been following your messes."

He explained how he had set out to follow them and each time he had thought he would catch up, the townsfolk would tell the tales of their exploits and then point in the direction of their next destination. All George had to do was follow the news.

James grimaced. "I didn't think people would care once we left."

George laughed. "Folks don't forget things like ghosts and demons. Especially when someone is crazy enough to stand up to them."

"See James. You're a legend just like you always dreamed about." Sarah patted his shoulder.

"Wow. I can't believe you came all this way to see me again." James filled the cups with well water.

"How do you know I traveled to see YOU?"

George glanced at Sarah. She understood the hint and blushed again. As she ducked her head to avoid revealing herself, she found Carson beaming as if he were the one who George had chosen to follow. Sarah giggled into the back of her hand.

James and Carson began arguing over who was more important in the George admiration society. The argument quickly ceased once Sarah placed the plates of food before them. All three males readied to dig in without saying prayers. Sarah clucked her tongue, signaling her expectations. James and Carson immediately dropped their forks and bowed their heads.

George stared at Sarah.

"Around here, we say thanks like proper folk before we start devouring our food." She narrowed her eyes and raised her brow. George let the piece of meat in his mouth fall back onto the plate. Sarah winced at his lack of decorum; although, she was grateful he had understood her wishes. She led the prayer and then thought she should quickly add in some other rules since George was new to their home.

"Before I forget, there is no spitting in this house. And bathing is highly encouraged."

Carson giggled.

George began eating rapidly as if he hadn't had a meal in quite some time. "I won't spit in the house."

Sarah wondered if that meant he had agreed to one set of terms and not the other. She would have to mention talking with a mouth full of food next time. Sarah knew men were rough around the edges and required home breaking. She realized her struggles with James and Carson had been nothing compared to the brutish, wild standards George had been accustomed to his whole life. Changing a man was one project she didn't mind working on.

"So, George. How long are you going to stay with us?"

Sarah had wondered the same thing. She turned her attention from James to George. He used his tongue to tuck the meat into his cheek.

"I guess it depends how long I'm wanted around here."

Sarah felt her skin redden. She traded looks with George who never took his eyes off her. She felt like a young girl again, being chased after by the boy in the yard. Sarah liked the attention George had been paying her. But she still found it strange to think of George in such a manner.

"We have lots of work on the farm. Could always use another set of hands to help with the chores." James finished a drink of water. "We wouldn't be able to pay you though. So we understand if you wish to move on."

George used the back of his sleeve to wipe his mouth. Sarah bit her lip to keep from pointing it out to him.

"Suppose we can work out other arrangements until you can afford to pay me."

Sarah kept her eyes fixed on her plate. She was afraid to reveal her understanding of George's hint.

"What do you think, Mom? Can we keep him?" James brimmed with excitement.

Sarah suddenly felt as if the world had begun to move too fast. She needed to get a grip on the situation before she found herself in the middle of even more changes in her life. She had finally begun to get settled into their new home.

"I don't know, James. Where would he sleep?" She stiffened as soon as she said it, afraid the answer would be her bed.

"No problem. He can take my room. And I'll move into Carson's room." James slammed his fist on the table like he had just solved a crisis of national importance.

Carson cheered, happy to have James near his side once again.

Sarah witnessed the pleading in both of their eyes. She turned to George and shrugged, unsure of what to say next.

George smiled.

"That works for now."

Sarah wondered what she had just gotten into.

CHAPTER 11

Just a few hours after the reunion had ended and everyone had fallen into a peaceful slumber, the night erupted into a din of horrific shrieks. Carson bolted upright in his bed. He pulled his blanket in front of his face and flattened himself against the wall, afraid of what might come through the window for him.

James groaned and rolled up to his knees before the window.

"Screeper." Carson croaked the word through his blanket. "Screeper."

"What the hell IS this thing?" James stared into the darkness. The pitch-black night was void of any moon glow.

Carson trembled. He imagined the monstrosity standing just beyond the window frame. Its hulking frame flared as its massive lungs breathed in massive gulps of air. Spiked fangs, dripping with saliva and blood, tilted out toward James as it prepared to feed on his flesh.

"I'm gonna get to the bottom of this once and for all." James began to pull on his dungarees. He lost his balance as one foot caught on the waistband. He fell onto Carson's bed.

Carson dug his nails into James' neck.

"Don't go, James." He started to cry. He felt ashamed of how his fear took hold of his emotions. He didn't want James to think he was a baby.

"I'll be alright. I got my gun." James tried to peel Carson's hands from his skin.

The thought of the Screeper snatching James off the ground and drinking his blood brought fresh tears to Carson's eyes.

"No. No."

James freed himself and continued to pull his dungarees up. "Carson, I promise. Ain't nothing I can't handle. Look at all we've been through."

Carson slammed his eyes closed. He remembered the haunted gunslinger and his own wounds. Preacher and the destruction left behind. The loss of their good friend, Crouching Bear.

Even the loss of his mother.

"What if your luck runs out?" Carson whispered into his blanket. He froze as the words crept through his lips, surprised he could say such a thing.

Think such a thought.

James chuckled. "You've taught me luck can't ever run out when we play cards." He ruffled Carson's hair then began to slip on his boots.

"That's not luck. I pay attention. You never pay attention." Carson raised his voice, frustration lacing his words. He wondered why James wouldn't listen to him. Carson knew James was stubborn, but this wasn't the time to be brave. Or foolish. Carson felt something very wrong was going to happen. The sensation gurgled in his belly. He choked back a feeling of getting sick all over his bed.

James finished slipping on his boots. He made his way for the door. Carson leapt from the bed and tugged on the back of James' pants. His hands slid down and Carson found himself wrapped around one of James' legs.

"Carson. Enough. I gotta go." James tried to shake Carson from his limb. He tore Carson free and shoved him to the floor. Carson grew angry with how violently James had tossed him away.

James opened the bedroom door and ran smack into a wall.

George stood in the hallway, wearing his red, one-piece undergarment. And boots.

"Seems like old times." George grinned. "Let's go kill some monsters."

"I retired from that line of work. That's why we came here."

George laughed. "I'd say that was a good choice. You weren't any good at it anyway."

Carson tucked himself between the men. They both stared down at him.

"Don't go. Please." He pleaded for James to listen to him.

James ignored Carson. He stomped to the kitchen. George followed closely behind, brushing past Carson.

Soft but strong hands clutched Carson's shoulders from behind. He froze, scared the Screeper had sneaked in the bedroom window to attack him. Carson realized it was Sarah when he caught a whiff of her pretty soap smell.

"What's all the noise about?"

Carson pointed at James and George. He knew he had to tell on them for their own good. "They're getting hurted by the Screeper."

Sarah squeezed his flesh.

"What are you going to do?" Sarah moved around Carson, stepping into the kitchen.

James and George exchanged glances.

"We're fixing to rid a beast." George tucked a chunk of chewing tobacco into the corner of his mouth.

"Not in my house, Mister." Sarah pointed at George. He lowered his eyes, nodded gently and stepped outside. "James, you're scaring Carson."

"I'M not scaring Carson. That...that...thing is what's scaring him."

Carson grasped Sarah's hand. He contemplated joining James and George on their quest to hunt down the Screeper. But, as quickly as he considered it, Carson dropped the notion because of his fear of what creature stalked the plains beyond their homestead. He wanted to beg James to stay home and wait until daylight before going after the monster. The arguments jumbled in his brain as he fought off the terror in his chest.

"Please be careful, James."

Carson buried his face in Sarah's nightdress. She had given in to James and George. He had failed to convince them to stay inside. And

Sarah hardly backed him up. He whimpered into the folds of her clothing. If anything happened to James, Carson decided he would run away from home. He wouldn't be able to face Sarah for letting James walk into his own death.

Without James, Carson reasoned he would have little to live for. He loved Sarah like his own mother. But James was his whole world. He shuddered to think about life without his best friend to talk to. Who would protect him? Who would play cards with him?

Carson watched James walk out the door. It slammed behind him. He waited for the sound of the Screeper tearing apart his only friend.

A horrific scream shook the walls of the ranch.

Carson bolted for his room. He grabbed his blanket, wrapped it around himself tightly and rolled under his bed frame. He scrunched his back against the wall. Carson left a tiny opening before his eyes so he could watch for the Screeper's hooves as it stalked through his room in search of his blood.

Another shriek outside.

Carson pulled the blanket closed so the Screeper wouldn't find him.

CHAPTER 12

The darkness cloaked their steps, cloying at their backs like an unseen, bony hand. They had stuck together, figuring they stood a better chance of surviving. Safety in numbers. James wondered if two men were enough against the thing that haunted their farm. It sounded much bigger and fiercer than anything he had faced before.

James trembled. He tried to remember how he had remained so brave against Crouching Bear and the gunslinger. Maybe his naivety had carried him through those battles.

Or maybe he was wiser now. Had more to lose these days.

George stooped to the earth. He felt along the scrub brush. James watched his friend lower his face to the ground. George sniffed loudly. He looked around the field before standing to face James.

"I found a track."

James wished he could learn George's skills. "And?"

"It's big. Ain't no coyote track." George spat tobacco juice. "Smells like death."

His stomach curled. James swallowed, tasting the pasty sleep on the back of his tongue.

George began following the path of the paw prints. James hurried behind him. They snaked along the farm as the tracks seemed to meander across the land in a haphazard trail. James felt the hairs on the back of his neck stand on end. He sensed they were being watched. Maybe stalked. He turned to check the way they had come for something creeping up on them.

Nothing.

James spun to catch up with George and ran smack into the back of the large man. George shushed James, pushing him back with a tree-trunk of a forearm. James stared at him, trying to figure out what George had found.

"Hear that?"

James trained his ears. The nervous shifting of the animals in the pen is all James heard.

"I don't hear anything."

"Exactly. Nothing. Ain't no screams since we came out." George spat.

"Think it's gone?" James gulped, listening for a sneak attack.

George remained stoic. He shook his head slightly. "Dunno."

James wanted to go check on his animals. Their stressful sounds brought him back to his true purpose. He had to protect his farm and family.

He should've listened to the locals. Scoffing at the stories and rumors may have been a mistake.

"I'm gonna see to the pen. We can check again in the morning. It's too dark out here." James began to head back.

"Go ahead. I'll catch up with you."

"Where are you going? It's too dangerous by yourself."

George spat a plume of juicy tobacco. "I want to make a full pass along the edge, son. You go on."

James bristled. "I'm not your son."

Before James could give more attitude to George, the large man cut him off. "You're lucky. If you were, I'd tan your hide for endangering your mother."

George disappeared into the inky blackness. James bit his lower lip. He wanted to punch George in the nose for talking down to him as if he were a little child. He hadn't endangered them. Or had he? James sulked. It was his fault they had bought the farm and settled where others had warned them not to. He had allowed a good deal and his own ego of becoming the provider and protector to cloud his judgment.

James kicked at the dirt on his way up to the pen. He kept his head on a swivel in case anything should lunge from the shadows. The gate to the pen was still closed. He lifted the handle and stepped inside. All the animals huddled at the back of the fence, closer to the house. James recognized Tina's girth obliterating the rest of the pigs and goats who hid behind her massive rump. James softly whistled as he approached, letting Tina and the others know it was him nearing. Tina grunted. He rubbed her spine, trying to assure her of the safety, even if he didn't feel safe himself. Tina's skin prickled with gooseflesh. James knew she was as spooked as he was.

He cooed and spoke in whispered tones to reassure Tina. She lowered her head into his stomach, nuzzling against him. The kids bayed, happy to have James as protection. He scratched at the furry little scalps.

The scent hit him suddenly.

It was a stench James had known well but he refused to become accustomed to it.

Death.

James left the animals in the corner of the pen. He shuffled toward the east, following the smell that bit at his nostrils. He felt his gorge threaten to rise. James knelt over a clump in the dirt. With no light, James found his hand reaching for the dead creature before him. Just as his hand neared the corpse, a bright flash of light blinded his eyes.

George stood over the corner of the fence with a lit match. The small glow of light brought the horror to their eyes.

One of the pigs was decimated.

It had been the second largest pig, Jasper. The body was shredded into pieces. James found it strange that the limbs and torso were still intact. Just not attached to each other. Nor the head. The mouth hung open in a cry of horror. Both eyes were gone from the skull. The tongue was missing too.

And there was no blood. Anywhere.

"What the?" George grumbled.

James turned the legs over. The meat intact, but the ends which had been separated from the body were yellowed. Only fatty tissue showed where there should have been blood seeping from the open wounds. It looked as if the blood had been sucked dry from the body parts.

The cuts along the flesh were nearly clean as well, like a surgeon had cut the limbs with surgical precision.

What kind of beast could do such a thing? Were they up against an animal or a man? It couldn't have been a man. The shrieks, so ungodly and foreign. Surely those sounds could only have come from something that had been spawned by hell. Nothing from this earth.

James dropped the leg into the dirt. He brushed his hand off on his pants. "We have to keep this to ourselves. We can't scare Carson any more than he is already."

George cleared the chaw from the inside of his cheek. He flicked the wad of leaf to the ground. "I've never seen anything like this in my life."

James thought he saw something in George's eyes that he had never thought he would live to see.

Worry. And fear.

CHAPTER 13

James stepped onto the porch. The day promised to be a hot one as the early morning temperature flirted with the low 80's. He gulped in the thick, fresh air, squinting against the blazing glare.

He had slept little last night. After the screams and the horrific discovery of Jasper's remains, James had found restlessness and anguish instead of slumber. It took him quite some time to coax Carson from his hiding spot beneath the bed. The poor boy had been inconsolable. James found himself frustrated with Carson's inability to grasp reality. At one point, James had wanted to slap the whiny attitude from Carson's face. He felt guilty for losing patience with the boy. Carson wasn't an ordinary kid. He saw the world through the mind of a child much younger than his age. And he would always be that way. How would James react to Carson when he became an adult in size and age, but remained a child in mind? Would he wish to punish his friend for things out of his control then too? James tried to forget his almost violent behavior.

The idea he came up with was to sneak out early this morning and hunt for clues as to the creature that tormented their peaceful lives. He wanted to find the creature so he could rid them of their problems. James worried about what he would find in his search. The rumble of the screams shook the house walls, his lungs inside his chest, his confidence. He imagined an animal with enormous fangs and claws like cutlass blades. The visions quaked along his spine.

James hurried down the porch to the yard. He checked his revolver as he trotted, making sure all six chambers were filled with lead. James shoved the gun into his waistband and scoured the horizon for signs of something that didn't belong.

He slowed up outside the pen. Tina grunted and shoved her nose through a fresh slop of filth. The rest of the pigs rolled around in the muck, a few wrestling each other to establish pecking order. The goats laid in a semi-circle, staring at James as if they waited with bated breath for him to preach the gospel to them. The chickens clucked and pecked at tiny morsels along the dirt. They carried on like James wasn't even there. He smiled to himself. He loved his animals.

James traced the path he and George had set out upon the previous evening. Twenty yards later, he spied the huge paw print George had discovered. It was five or six inches wide and at least twice that in length. What really shook James was the depth of the track. It had sunk into the soil a good two inches or so. He understood how big a creature it would take to create such an impression on compact, hard soil. The surmised weight of the beast hinted at its enormity.

Every few feet another paw print revealed its path. James easily followed along the course as it circled back toward the pen and off to the rock outcropping. James thought it was odd how the tracks ceased before it neared the pen. If it hadn't gotten as far as the fence line then how did it kill Jasper? Had the animal jumped from afar and cleared the waist-high fencing? James scratched his stubble, pondering such a potential feat. He continued along the trail until it seemed to die off on its trajectory near the rocks. The earth revealed a large smear of chaos, prints intermingled and overstepping each other. Many smaller prints danced here and there. The larger prints died off amid the turmoil. He brushed a sheen of sweat from his upper lip as he took in the scene, trying to determine where the things had come from. And where they had gone to.

There was more than one.

Knots tightened in his chest. James hadn't prepared himself to fight an army of deadly monsters. He had assumed the howling they had heard on prior nights had been a pack of coyotes. Maybe he had been wrong. Perhaps it was a pack of something far scarier. Or it could be a pack of coyotes who followed an unearthly abomination, feeding on the scraps it left behind. James knew coyotes were opportunistic. They traveled in packs so they could gang up on their prey. They were just as lazy though, making it a possibility that they lingered in the shadows of something that left behind food.

It left the whole animal behind though. Not scraps. The only thing missing was the blood. What on earth would suck the blood from its kill and not chew the meat?

James didn't want to answer his own question.

He rounded the outcropping, finding a few piles of scat along the edge. A few traces of prints picked up on the far side. James kept his head down and followed as best he could. The plains sloped away into a shallow valley that James hadn't realized was there. He thought about the times he had scouted the property and the nearby lands, and this had been the furthest he had traveled in this direction. The valley ended along a tree line.

A wooded lot rose up to the sky. Unlike everything else along the plain, the wooded copse looked plush and green like an oasis in the desert. James hunched his back and slowed his pace on approach. His stomach tightened at what might be hiding inside the woods. He pulled his gun from his waist, holding it casually in front of his body.

James noticed the shakiness in his hand.

He proceeded through the dense foliage, stepping carefully over a deadfall.

Something moved to his right. James stopped in his tracks. He squinted in the region of the noise. A small branch danced as if it had been brushed by something which had hurried off. James cocked the hammer on his revolver and stepped closer. Cautiously. He moved a few limbs away from his face with his free hand. He froze in place. The area he stared at appeared unnatural. It didn't quite fit in with the surrounding vegetation. Just as James raised his pistol at the strange shape, the plant blinked.

"Don't shoot."

James recognized the voice immediately. George. A plume of tobacco juice shot from the center of the shrub. George raised up to his feet, towering over James.

"I could've killed you." James lowered his gun. He relaxed. Then he grew angry that George had scared him.

"Why are you all...garnished like that?"

George smiled, his blackened teeth appearing white in the midst of all the greenery adorning his face and head. "If you want to hunt and kill your prey, you gotta get in their mind."

James huffed. "We ain't hunting a raspberry bush, dang it."

"I mean, you gotta get down to their level. See what they see. Think what they think."

James shook his head. "What we're hunting isn't down that low. Trust me. It's much bigger."

"But it ain't looking for greens. It's looking for meat. If you hide your shape then you can get close without it knowing you're there."

James realized George had a good point. His mind shifted to the surrounding woods. "Anything?"

George spat. He shook his head. "Not yet."

James sighed. "Let's get into town. We need to pick up some stuff to help us."

CHAPTER 14

Carson circled the pen. He liked to rile up the animals, running around the enclosure, singing out loud and dragging a stick along the fencing. The scratching sound of wood on wood made the goats run to the opposite side of the pen. The pigs, especially Tina, would oink and stomp their hooves. The chickens only reacted if they found themselves in the way of the other creatures.

The heat felt good along Carson's face and arms, a stark contrast to the chilly night air that crept into his bedroom window. He butchered the lyrics of Amazing Grace, pleased with creating his own song since he had forgotten the words to the original tune.

He tapped the stick upon the gate to the beat of his dance. Tina expressed her displeasure with a bluff charge and several deep grunts. Carson laughed. He enjoyed when the animals joined him in his fun. Carson swung his stick high above his head in a swirling motion. It slipped from his sweaty hand, landing ten feet behind him.

"Uh-oh. That was funnied."

Carson held up a finger, promising Tina and the others he would be right back. He ran to pick up his stick. As he bent to retrieve it, Carson noticed an indentation in the dirt. He crouched down and traced his finger along the edge of the paw print.

It was huge.

He felt an urge to pee but ignored it in favor of his new interest. The unsettling fear of the Screeper was challenged by a hint of bravery. Carson thought of the adventures he and James had dreamed about. They had planned to travel the country in search of bad guys. James would fight evil and save the good townsfolk from monsters and men in black hats. All the while, Carson would stand at James' side. Together, they would be victorious.

Carson realized he had been shirking his responsibility. He was supposed to help James. Instead, he had been cowering under the bed like a baby. Maybe he could prove himself to James, get back his best friend's confidence in his abilities to meet adventure, head on.

With an ambivalent pit in his stomach, Carson glared in the direction of the paw print. He crawled along the ground, kicking up clouds of dust, scouring the soil for the next marker. It didn't take long for him to locate another print. This one was shallow with ambiguous edges.

He stood and looked back toward the ranch. Sarah had told Carson to stay close to the house. She wanted him to be safe as she fixed a chair. Sarah said James and George had gone into town and they wouldn't be back for several hours. He realized he had strayed away from the house. He didn't want Sarah to get mad at him, but the sense of adventure tugged at his emotions.

Carson watched Sarah work.

"I'll be right back." Carson spoke aloud as if Sarah could hear him from this distance.

He returned his attention to the ground. Carson hurried along a fading trail of prints, drifting off toward a big pile of boulders. The adventure of tracking the Screeper disappeared. Carson wanted to climb the rocks instead. He missed climbing. Where they lived in Texas, there weren't many trees for Carson to climb. He loved climbing up trees or mounds of dirt. Carson had plenty of things to climb back in Iowa and Kansas. But this place was flat.

As he reached the top of the largest rock, Carson raised his hands to the sky like he had conquered the enemy. He could hardly see the farm from where he was. It looked like a small toy. He shouted as loud as he could, feeling free and happy for the first time since they had moved to the new homestead.

DESERT FANGS

Carson shielded his eyes from a blinding glint along the plain. Something shiny had caught the sunshine at just the right angle. He wondered if he had discovered a treasure chest full of gold and silver. Carson hurried down from the rocks to chase down his new interest. From the ground level, Carson struggled to find the object which had shined in the sun. As he searched for the potential treasure, Carson found a crumpled hat. The tanned fabric had softened and decayed with its exposure to the elements. The brim, no longer maintaining its original shape, sagged and wrinkled under the weight of dirt. Carson shook the hat, freeing the remnants of forgotten time. He held the hat aloft, inspecting the open crown and low brim. He wondered who had lost their hat and why they had allowed the hat to go missing for so long.

He remembered the treasure and decided to figure out the story behind the hat later. Carson scoured the earth for anything shiny. A small cross made of splintered wood leaned eastward as if the winds had pointed it toward an imaginary destination. Broken glass from an empty whiskey bottle sprinkled among the weeds like fragmented memories. Carson picked up a sliver of broken glass. He ran his finger along its beveled edge, tearing his skin. Carson immediately dropped the shard, squeezing his bloody fingertip. He winced against the pain, blowing air through his lips to keep himself from crying out.

Then he saw it.

A gold chain, thin and dusty, swung from one of the arms of the wooden cross. A tiny knot in the wood held the chain in place, preventing it from sliding completely off. At the end of the chain, a small Christian cross dangled. Carson touched the gold cross with his bloody finger. He grasped the chain, releasing it from its perch. Carson had never held real gold in his hands before. The delicate metal felt strange. He couldn't wait to tell James about the treasure he had found.

Treasure.

Carson suddenly remembered the wooden cross. His stomach sank. He had uncovered a grave site. On their property. Carson felt thousands of bugs crawling beneath his skin. The thought of a dead person in his vicinity gave him the creeps. He dropped the gold chain and started to run for the house.

He stopped after a few paces. How could he leave the gold behind for someone else to find? Carson had found it so now it would be his own. He scrambled to pick up the chain.

As he bent to grab it, Carson felt as if he were being watched. The hairs along the back of his neck stood on end. Carson spun in a circle, searching for the penetrating eyes he felt along his flesh.

Rather than waiting to see the Screeper, Carson snatched the gold chain and ran for the ranch. He ran as fast as he could, setting an all-time personal record for speed. Carson wouldn't allow the Screeper to catch him today.

CHAPTER 15

The alpha watched as the boy danced around the fenced area. While the animals inside the pen avoided the boy's antics, the beast found itself drawn to the child. It swallowed the excess saliva that grew inside its mouth, a reaction to a new potential meal.

Something about the boy fascinated the alpha male.

Surely, a youth of his size wouldn't make much of a full course. But the kill would be simpler to pull off.

The boy seemed off.

The alpha was adept at judging its surroundings. Harsh lessons had taught it to optimize the killing, choosing the best moments to strike, identifying the circumstances which would lead to its best chances for survival. Identifying the weakest members of the pack. Or the prey.

And the humans.

It sensed the defects in the boy. A certain...slowness.

The alpha grinned, allowing a long, slimy drip of saliva to free itself from its maw.

The boy gave up the singing and dancing. He lowered himself to the ground, crawling along the earth like the animals it tormented in the pen. The boy slithered along the dirt like a snake, whispering and searching for something. Perhaps the boy had lost his toys.

Or his way.

Hopefully.

The beast deliberated whether it needed to hide its newfound target from the pack. The others grew hungrier with each passing day. They foolishly believed themselves to be on the same level as the alpha. A mistake which must be reinforced periodically. But they knew they owned the real power. Numbers.

The alpha stifled a roar of disgust. It wanted to cry out in rage against the hackled creatures that followed it around. Maggots. They existed to feed off the scraps left behind. And to fight for dominance over the pack. Dominance the alpha had won over. Using fearless tenacity and lots of blood. Its own blood.

The boy ran along the plain. He headed toward the throne. The alpha's throne. The outcropping of rock served as the alpha's dais, the symbol of its authority as it ruled over the rest of the dogs.

It shuffled low, pressing its haunches to the earth to conceal its travel. The fur provided a camouflaged backdrop to the surrounding environment. It lurked nearby, close enough to smell the delightful fragrance of the unwashed little boy, yet far enough to protect against discovery.

The alpha sniffed the air, inquiring if its brothers had aroused from their slumber to find their leader missing. They would come in search of him, hoping to wander into an easy dinner at the feet of the sated leader. No signs of the pack were detected. The alpha set its sights on the new residents of the farm. After slaughtering the animals of the prior owner, one by one, and finishing off the owner himself, the pack had returned to the plains for smaller, less filling food. Bunnies, squirrels and other rodents did little to stave off the hunger pangs. The foxes and bobcats provided more meat but were wise enough to migrate away from this territory in order to survive.

Now, the alpha wanted to return to larger prey. Humans. The taste of human flesh and blood was like a fine delicacy. The fight each human put up made the killing more satisfactory too. Any beast could dispatch a small rodent. But to take the life of a farmer or cowpoke, a formidable foe with weapons and a strong survival instinct became quite an event.

A blood sport.

The boy shouted from the highest rock. It grizzled the alpha to allow the child to disrespect its throne of authority. However, the time wasn't right. The alpha would punish the boy for mocking its superiority. It would slowly drain the child's blood, watching the boy struggle to breathe, drowning in his own gore. Then the alpha would devour each limb as the boy watched his body consumed by the hulking mass. Each time the boy began to fade into unconsciousness, the alpha would prod the child to stay focused on his eventual passing. The alpha would bray at the moon, summoning the rest of the pack to their missed opportunity and warning all other creatures, near and far, of the new and reigning lord of the plains.

It slavered a sticky tongue along drooling fangs. The attention returning to the slow boy who climbed down from the throne. He hurried back in the direction of the farm, turning his back to the beast. The primal instincts kicked in, presenting an overwhelming urge to chase its prey and pounce upon the flesh of the young. The alpha fought the instinct, nestling down as quickly as it arose to follow through on its ancestral survival tactics. Once again, the beast skulked low, shielding itself from detection, as it slowly followed the scent of the boy.

The child discovered the grave of the prior farmer. The one who had bravely stood his ground against the impossible odds. The old man who had weathered so many hardships through a difficult life, only to be plucked away without so much as a hesitancy toward escape. To stay alive. The old man had perished because of an ego, an unchecked belief carried by all humans, that they held dominion over four-legged beasts. A fallacy which had been proven over countless millennia by creatures big and small.

But none before had deserved the title, the responsibility, of becoming the most formidable devil to walk the earth. An animal that lived on instinct yet reasoned as a more upright being. A creature so entrenched in killing and bloodshed.

The child would live. Today. But soon, the alpha would pick the bones clean. It would swill the organ juices and slurp the vitriolic fluids. The beast would commune with the holiest spirit in Hell as it brought an apocalypse to the fair folks of the plain. And once it had fed upon the humans, there would be no more turning back. No pack to serve.

Nothing to stand between its wicked cravings and the domination of all living things.

The alpha was a one-of-a-kind creation. It understood how special it was.

And now the rest of the world would understand as well.

CHAPTER 16

James had grown frustrated with the folks in town. He had come to stock up on supplies, bullets and trapping materials, as well as some extra feed for the animals. But he also wanted to learn more about the farm. Folks had openly entreated him not to buy the property, sharing all kinds of theories. They tried to scare him with gory details of the old man who had owned the farm.

Now, they were all tight-lipped.

He had started at the General Store. Then the Barber Shop. He'd even stopped people in the street several times, asking anyone who looked as if they had an honest face. However, the residents complained they were in a hurry, or they swore up and down they had never heard of such stories. One lady hollered at James for spreading rumors. She accused James of sinning because he gossiped about his neighbors. Before James could argue that he had never known the old farmer, George had restrained him with a firm grasp of the shoulder.

"I ain't seen so many people try to avoid me like this."

George smirked. "Maybe you should wash up." He faked a few sniffs at the air around James.

James shoved at George. The large man didn't even budge. James removed his hat and scratched at his sweaty head. He knew time was short and he needed to return to the farm to finish out the day with some work. As he peered around the town, George stuffed some tobacco inside his cheek. He offered the pouch to James. Thinking he should grow up and become more of a man, James jammed his hand into the pouch and pulled an enormous fistful of tobacco.

"You chewing all that at once? Or saving up for a rainy day?" George glared at him.

James looked at his hand and wondered how he could fit it all in his mouth. George ripped a clump of it away from him, tucking it back into his pouch. James nodded at George and filled his cheeks with the juicy leaves. The flavor was interesting, almost sweet. Then James swallowed.

His stomach knotted and lurched. James bent in the middle of the street, spitting out the tobacco. He gagged several times but managed to save his gorge from punching a whole in the top of his head.

"How do you eat that junk?" James choked. "That's disgusting."

George laughed and slapped James' back. "The trick is to chew it, not eat it."

James spat. The awful flavor of stomach acid and pungent weeds filled his mouth. He spat again but the taste lingered like an outhouse aroma. He pointed at the saloon across the street.

"I need a sarsaparilla to clean my mouth. Then we'll hit the road."

George mocked James. "You think you're man enough to handle a stiff drink like that?"

James glowered at George. He knew his friend was busting his chops, but his disappointment with the locals and his bout with the chewing tobacco left James in a surly mood. As they entered the saloon, James sidled up to the bar. A group of men occupied most of the space, forcing James to shimmy in between. A tall man in a black hat jammed his elbow into James' side. James stepped into the man, staring up into his face.

"Problem, boy?" The man's friends broke into laughter. They cheered on their large friend for the fight they hoped would break out. James never took his eyes from the man.

"I want a sarsaparilla. And then I'm leaving your crappy little town."

The men laughed harder. James knew he had worsened his situation by ordering a child's drink. He bristled at not ordering a whiskey instead.

George pushed James aside. He stood toe to toe with the large man. One of the men standing at the bar commented how James' father had to fight his battles. The men chuckled. George picked up the man's shot glass, spat his tobacco juice in it and handed it to the man. The large man glared at the personal afront in his hand. He slammed the glass upon the bar and began to cock his fist back to strike George.

James lunged forward. His forehead connected with the large man's nose, exploding with a thunderous crack and a spray of blood. The man dropped to the floor, clutching his ruined face. Two men stepped up as if they would come to the aid of their fallen friend. The others slid into the background, avoiding any hassles.

"We don't want any trouble. Just a drink and then we're leaving." James rubbed his reddening head with the back of his hand. "He started it." James pointed at the man on the floor. As soon as he said it, James blushed for sounding like a child again.

The bartender slammed a bottle of sarsaparilla on the counter. He looked at George, awaiting his choice of drink. George ignored the bartender and leaned against the bar. James tossed a silver coin on the counter. He grabbed the bottle and downed half the liquid in three gulps. The brew masked a bit of the taste in his mouth, but not enough to settle his stomach.

"Does anybody in this town know what happened at the farm out west?"

The bartender glanced around the saloon. He leaned closer to James and spoke in a hushed tone. "Something ungodly out there."

James took another swig. He placed the bottle down. "What killed the farmer? Nobody will tell me what happened. But I know everyone knows."

The bartender tidied up with his rag. He glanced around again, ensuring their conversation was private.

"Nobody seen it. Only a monster could do what that thing done."

The bartender backed away to refill some whiskeys.

James clenched his fists. He needed to get back to the farm before he lost his temper with the secretive residents of town. James gulped the rest of his bottle. He stomped for the door, hearing George follow close behind. James stepped into the street. He paused and exhaled a long, exasperated breath.

"I would give anything to find out what killed that farmer."

"Anything?"

James spun to find the strange voice. Sitting along the saloon porch was a Mexican with a large-brimmed sombrero. The man spoke again. James couldn't see the man's face as his head remained low, covered by the large hat.

"I know something about your problem." The Mexican looked up at James. He smiled, a toothless grin, shocking James and George.

"But it will cost you."

CHAPTER 17

The man's tanned skin was covered in a thin film of dust. Even his wispy mustache and chin beard were coated in filth. James wondered how a man could allow himself to become so gritty without it bothering his skin. He'd encountered travelers and known mountain men who had smelled as if they had bathed in the droppings of beasts. But this man took his grime to a whole new level. James held his breath as he stood before the diminutive Mexican.

"My name is Miguel Herrera Juan Pablo Rodriguez. But you can call me Miguelito." He tilted the wide brim of his hat away from his dark eyes. A gentle hand raised along his cheek as if he had a secret to divulge. "My close friends call me Lito."

James shot a glance at George.

"We ain't friends yet, compadre." George grumbled and spat.

"Oh, very good, senor. You speak my tongue, eh?"

George moved his chaw from one side of his mouth to the other. James feared George would rip the man in two. He stepped in between the men to dissuade George from aggression.

"What do you know about the farm?"

Lito chuckled. As he laughed, his rotund belly jiggled beneath his soiled shirt.

"I told you. It will cost you."

George shoved James aside. "Maybe it'll cost YOU for mouthing off."

Lito continued to chuckle but scampered behind James in fear of the large man.

James spun to face Lito again. "What is your price?" George grunted until James rested his palm along his chest.

"Well now. Today is your lucky day, mi amigo. You see? I am on sale for a low, low price, eh?"

James narrowed his eyes. The Mexican was a bit too playful. He wondered if the man was just stringing him along, or if he had real information about the previous owner of the farm. James heard an echo of Carson's words in the back of his mind.

Pay attention.

James warmed to the notion he might be able to channel his little friend's gamesmanship to get what he needed out of Lito.

"Price." James barked in Lito's face.

"Twenty American dollars." Lito rubbed his palms together.

"Forget it." James turned on his heels. He knew the man was attempting to extort a large sum of money from him. And probably for nothing he could use to figure out what had happened on the farm before he had purchased the property.

"Ten. That is my final offer. And it is a bargain for you, mi amigo. Very cheap. Very cheap."

James nodded at George. George stepped toward Lito and grasped the smaller man's neckerchief. He quickly tightened the cloth until the cords were straining from the sides of Lito's neck. The small man lifted slightly off the floorboards outside the saloon.

"Wait." Lito squeaked the words. Some spittle dotted his dried lips. "Wait."

James nodded at George, signaling the big man to release his grip. George dropped Lito to the ground in cloud of dust. Lito gasped for air. He coughed into the soil and rolled around as if he had been shot. James wanted to laugh at the unseemly antics but he contained his amusement in order to secure the best deal. Or at least to squeeze whatever knowledge the drifter had out of his cunning head.

"Okay. Okay. You are good businessman. I like you, mi amigo." Lito brushed the sand from his face. "Five dollars."

James walked away. He felt angry with himself for believing he could get somewhere with the vagrant. Part of him wanted to pistol whip the man back across the border from which he had come. But he'd rather leave than waste another minute with the wretched soul.

As James and George approached their horses, Lito came hustling after them. He called out to get one more chance at negotiating an arrangement they could mutually benefit from. George climbed upon his steed. James began to swing his leg over his own horse when Lito tugged at his pant leg.

"Wait." Lito bent to catch his wind. His stout build had struggled to keep pace with them. "Don't you want to know what it is? Aren't you curious to find out about the secret that nobody wants to whisper?"

James glared down at Lito. "I'm interested in knowing things. But I have no interest in playing games with you. Or being taken advantage of. I'm not a kid."

George snorted.

James ignored George's mockery. He bristled at how childish the statement had ended up sounding once it had passed his lips. James tugged the reins and clicked his tongue to get the horse moving. Lito hurried after them as they trotted away.

"El Chupacabra!"

James stopped his horse. George kept his horse trotting along a few more paces before he pulled short as well.

"A what?"

"El Chupacabra." Lito shucked his wide-brimmed hat from his head and fanned the heat from his face. He bent to rest his hands on his knees, trying to catch his breath.

"Is that Mexican for asking for a whooping?" George leaned over to grit his teeth menacingly at Lito.

"El Chupacabra. It is a monster."

James gulped. He hadn't understood the words Lito had spoken. But he understood the word 'monster.' Carson had said it. George had said it. And James had thought it. Lito now had James' attention.

"Why don't you climb up and come with us. You can tell us all about this...monster."

Lito made his way toward George. A thick splat of dark tobacco juice splashed along the dirt before Lito's feet. He stopped short to avoid the mess. Lito seemed to understand the gesture as he changed course for James' horse instead.

George pulled alongside James. He leaned close and spoke in a hushed tone. "You know what you're doing?"

James blinked. He thought he did but George's question made him second guess himself. James figured they could bring Lito to the farm and get the information they needed from him, far from prying eyes and ears in town. However, George's hesitation might be appropriate. What if Lito still had no information? Bringing him out to their home could endanger Sarah and Carson.

Or having Lito to themselves might be helpful. Nobody would hear his pleas if they had to coax the info from him in a more forceful manner.

James shook the evil thoughts from his mind. He realized he was far more capable of certain actions when it came to protecting his loved ones.

Hopefully, today would not be one of those days that required the side of James who battled the evils of the world.

CHAPTER 18

Sarah winced at the pain in her hand. She had been moving some of the furniture around in an attempt to get into every nook and cranny. Sarah kept a clean house but she had wanted to ensure the home was extra spotless.

For George.

She'd slid the bed frame back along the wall but Sarah hadn't moved her hand in time. The frame crunched her hand against the wall. Sarah stifled her surprise through gritted teeth. The last thing she needed was for Carson to hear her yelp. He'd come running to check on her, dragging all his dirt with him and creating brand new mess for her to tidy.

Sarah rubbed her sore fist as she inspected her work. She realized her desires were nonsense. She'd been acting like a schoolgirl ever since George had arrived. Never had Sarah thought of George as anything except a hulking, filthy man with dreadful habits and absent manners. Sure he had protected them against hooligans back in Iowa. But he'd also been a pain in her rump. George would keep after the ladies as if he were an auxiliary madame. His imposing figure would hint at Filler's intolerance, forcing the ladies to step it up in their cleaning and "customer service."

And now she was blushing at his presence, not to mention spending valuable time tending to inside chores when so much farm work needed to be done. Besides, Sarah reasoned, George was dirty. She knew all the cleaning in the world would be quickly undone as soon as the mammoth man crossed the threshold. He'd pat his dusty clothes and rub his body odor on the bedsheets. Sarah didn't even want to imagine what he was like in the outhouse.

Sarah swallowed the gorge that threatened to rise.

Yet, she had grown to think something else of George.

Possibilities.

Maybe she could finally find the love she had always longed for. Perhaps Sarah could provide the proper home life for her boys. Maybe she could change George, turning him into her own reclamation project.

Project indeed.

Sarah chuckled to herself.

Her mind made up, Sarah lifted her bucket and scrub brush. As she dumped the milky water over the porch railing, Sarah watched Carson teasing the animals. He circled the pen with a stick, singing an unknown song. She giggled at the out of tune cadence.

"Carson, quit bothering Tina before she chases you."

From across the yard, Carson's face wilted in fear. He had stopped dead in his tracks and stared at Sarah as he considered the danger in his taunting. Carson dropped his stick and ran toward her.

His breath came in gasps from sprinting to the porch.

"Will James be home soon?"

Sarah scanned the horizon. The men had been gone for quite some time. She knew they had to pick up more supplies and James had mentioned something about asking for help with whatever was tormenting their homestead at night.

"I hope so. The day is slipping away and we still have so much work to do."

Carson scrunched his nose. Sarah knew Carson would rather play than work. The mere mention of chores would send Carson into hiding. She hid her smile behind her hand.

"Tell you what. Why don't you take a bath and call it a day? But you must stay inside afterward. Not like that time you bathed and then went on an adventure. That was a complete waste of soap and water."

He narrowed his eyes in consideration of her suggestion. "But what if James comes home and we have to kill the Screeper?"

Sarah placed her hands on her hips. "There will be no more talk of Screepers and killing. You hear me? There's nothing out there but coyotes and prairie dogs. And even if there was, you wouldn't be going after it."

"Aw, but that's not faired. James and me are supposed to fight monsters together." Carson stomped his boot on the porch.

"James and George can handle it."

Carson crossed his arms over his chest and pouted. "I was here first. George isn't James' bested friend."

Sarah realized she had put a wedge between George and Carson. She tried to correct her error. "Well, I need a strong man to protect me while somebody chases the monsters. Would you rather George watch over me or you?"

Carson searched the sky in thought. Sarah couldn't stand how cute the boy could be. She wanted to pinch his cheeks and smother him with hugs every time he saw him.

"George can watched you. Me and James are a team. Not George." He nodded in exclamation to his final answer.

Sarah grinned. She tousled Carson's hair. "Alright. Well, we'll decide all that later. For now, I need you to go inside and take a bath. Make sure you scrub in between your toes and behind your ears." Sarah bent to meet Carson's eyes with her own. "I'm going to check how well you did and, if you aren't cleaned proper, then you will do it again."

Carson huffed and shuffled into the house. Sarah laughed.

Tina snorted. The sound startled Sarah. It made her think about the creature that haunted their nights. She worried about whatever the beast could be, and how long they could cope with its menacing visits before they'd have to pick up and move.

Or deal with the animal in a battle of survival.

She hoped James would return with bigger traps and information on what they'd been dealing with. As much as she loved their new life in Texas, part of Sarah wished she could return to the relative safety of the bigger towns they had come from. Men were dangerous but she felt as if she knew how to deal with them. The unknown of the wilderness was a different matter altogether. Absolute darkness at night and few neighbors to come to their aid brought chills to Sarah's flesh. Freedom came at a cost once you factored in the small things like helping hands.

Out here, they were on their own.

Sarah clutched at her throbbing hand. She stared across the land, searching for a set of eyes. Something that might be stalking her. Waiting for the perfect moment to strike. She took a deep breath and glanced back toward the trail, willing the sight of James and George coming back from town.

The path was quiet. She picked up her bucket and hurried inside to check on Carson's progress. But mostly to hide safely inside the four walls of the home.

CHAPTER 19

The alpha understood that time was short. It had paid careful attention to the pack. The others had grown bolder. Insurrection was close at hand.

Even the scent upon the wind had changed.

Soon, the bravest of the pack would make their move to unseat him. And he'd have to be swift and sure in his action. Pondering the strategy to beat down the defiance, the alpha had decided to make a complete break from the pack. Initially, he would wait, with one eye open, as they moved in for the kill. Then he would unleash the fires of hell upon the beasts.

However, it reveled in enjoying the game. It wouldn't be satisfying enough to lie in wait for the charge. Much more fun could be achieved in several parries and thrusts. Taunting the pack. Daring them to step forward in the face of danger.

He licked his chops to keep the saliva from escaping into the arid afternoon.

The alpha rose to its feet. It yawned, slowly stretching its maw to trick the rest into believing there was nothing to fear. It strode across the dust toward the creature who most figured to become the next alpha. In order to push their buttons, he knew he'd have to dispatch the next in line. It would force desperation and the pack would make their move under cover of night.

This fight would be more personal though.

The alpha stood before the next in line. He turned askew and watered the beast with a hard stream of piss. The beta jumped to its feet, snapping its jaws at him as it shook the urine from its coat.

A circle formed.

The alpha stepped back without a sound. The cacophony of barks and growls drowned out the sounds of the beta's anger. It continued to snap sharp teeth. It made several bluff charges at the alpha in order to trick him into exposing his next move.

Instead, he remained in waiting. With eyes focused on the beta, the alpha listened carefully to the circle around them. It remained cautious in the event that somebody else might decide to join the fray. Take advantage of the distraction. Or increase the odds of victory by ganging up on him.

The beta made its move. It charged in, nipping at the alpha's muzzle. However, the alpha had been quicker. He'd feinted to the right to avoid the attack. In many situations, the alpha would have countered with an attack of his own.

But he preferred to savor the moment.

The circle pushed from behind, closing in tighter to force a more productive battle. The alpha swept a paw at the crowd behind him. A razor-sharp claw caught an onlooker in the throat, releasing a spray of crimson. The animal howled in anguish and fell to the dirt. Even with fresh meat among them, the pack ignored the dying animal to focus on the frenzy before them.

The beta took advantage of the distraction and chomped along the alpha's hind leg. The fangs dug into his flesh, electric currents of pain zinging through the alpha's body. Rather than reveal his surprise, the alpha choked down his yelp. He decided to end the playful exchange and finish the fight before he suffered more injuries.

It lowered its head, a clear show of deference. The beta took the bait. It dove in for the winning bite only to find the alpha ready. He used a strong paw to tamp down the beta's head. His teeth sank into the skull of the beta, crunching through bone with a thunderous crack. The beta's body twitched and trembled as paralysis took over where synapses used to rule.

The frenzy continued unabated. The pack lathered with rage as death infiltrated its ranks. Fresh meals forced dripping mouths and frothy tongues.

The alpha stepped back to stare into the dying eyes of the beta. He wanted the animal to understand that it had lost the fight and would die a horrible death. Dispatching the creature too early would rob him of his spoils. He grinned at the dying animal, watching the truth of the moment wash over the beast's face. Blood poured down from the skull, clouding the sad eyes before him. Again, the alpha grinned, licking his lips to hint at his enjoyment of the pending delicacy.

He clamped down on the skull, sinking his long canines into the holes he had originally punctured. The salty discharge of brain matter oozed down his throat. It tasted delicious. The alpha crunched down tighter, collapsing bone and sinew, squirting the circle of onlookers with gore.

The circle quieted. The raucous barks and grunts died down to low growls and whimpers. The sounds of defeat pleased the alpha. But he was smart enough to understand it would be temporary. The pack would build up their courage and devise their plan for tonight. The alpha would be ready. But for now, he would drizzle the seeds of horror upon their ragged coats.

He stood on his hind legs, ignoring the sharp pain of his injury. The alpha swung his head around so the corpse in his maw would spray the circle with the scent of death and defeat. Greasy slop of brain and blood splattered the surrounding earth, leaving behind the horrific specters of wild struggles.

The crowd dispersed a few members at a time. To each corner of the ground, the creatures licked their chops and buried their faces in the shadows of the hot sun.

He lowered the corpse to the ground, then lifted his head in a victorious howl. The alpha made personal eye contact with each of the pack as a dire warning that they would be next. His chest puffed out with glory. And he wished the night would come quickly so he could continue the adrenaline surge of war. Alas, he'd have to wait until time slipped past like the life force in the animal at his feet.

The alpha settled down and drank heartily of the blood which flowed from the beta's head. He slurped loudly so the others would salivate as they watched on with hungry stares. The fluids drained from the beta, he moved toward the beast he had killed with his claws. Once more, the alpha settled in and drank from the animal's body, careful not to spare one drop of the bloody elixir. It would be a sin to waste what had been provided for his nourishment.

And it served as another sign of his dominance over the pack that wanted him dead.

CHAPTER 20

James decided to interrogate Lito before they arrived at the homestead. He thought better about bringing Lito directly home in case the information scared Carson and Sarah. In his mind, James would be able to control the narrative if he had the facts in advance. Finishing the ride home, he'd determine which information to reveal to his family.

And which parts he'd keep a secret.

They'd pulled off the trail and settled in the shade of some cottonwoods. James used the excuse of having to relieve himself, which proved to be reality once he climbed down from his horse. George had stood guard until James returned.

Lito wasted little time revealing what he knew. He had a way of speaking that James found entertaining. The stout man preferred to take the long way to get to the point. James ignored his impatience as he got caught up in the skills of the storyteller.

"A long time ago, traders brought goods from Mexico to the tropical islands in the Caribbean." Lito pronounced the country as Mehhico but James nodded in understanding.

"Before leaving one of the islands, a Famoso captain lost one of his crew members. They searched and searched until they found the man. He was muerto."

George grunted at Lito.

"It means dead. The man was dead. And they find he had a scared expression on his face. Like he had seen El Diablo. The devil himself."

James hung on every word. He waved his hand for Lito to continue.

"The body. It was as if it hadn't been touched. Nothing they could see at first. And then, the captain, he checked the neck of the man and he find bites on the dead man's throat. But no blood. Just holes in the throat."

Lito wrapped his stubby fingers around his own neck to accentuate his words. James noticed the calluses on the man's fingers. And lots of dirt beneath his fingernails.

"All men bleed." George folded his arms across his chest like he believed Lito to be lying.

Lito tipped his hat as if he was acknowledging a beautiful woman on the street.

"Si. All men bleed. But I never told you the man did not bleed. I only say they find him with no blood."

"No blood?" James leaned closer, enthralled with the tale.

"Si. No blood. It had been sucked out. Todo. That means all the blood."

James and George looked at each other. James understood the growing impatience in George's eyes. He prompted Lito to get to the monster.

"So it had been the monster then that killed the man?"

Lito nodded. "The captain, he send men into the jungle to find the killer. They find nothing. So this captain, he goes to ciudad and he asks every man who can kill with taking all the blood from a man. And not one man answer. All run away rapido. Then this captain, he shake small muchacho, threaten to kill him and all his Familia if he no tell the captain where to look."

"And?" James pounced on Lito as the man paused to catch his breath.

"And the boy, he cry and wet himself. But he tell this captain about El Chupacabra."

"What is this L-Chupa...?"

"Chupacabra. It is the monster that sucks the blood. It mean goat sucker."

George spat a plume of tobacco juice. "Goat sucker?"

"Si. In the islands, it mostly sucks the goats in the villages and fields. But it is hungry. It wants more blood."

James rubbed his temple. The heat was oppressive even in the shade. He wanted to get home but he remained fascinated with Lito's story.

"That's it? Some goat killer on a distant island is what we have?" George unsheathed his Bowie knife and held it aloft so a bit of light gleamed off the sharp steel. "I say we gut him now so we can get home for supper."

Lito jumped to his feet. His eyes grew wide with terror.

"Por favor, senor. It is truth. Why would I lie?"

James held up a hand to keep George at bay.

"What does your story have to do with what we are hunting?"

Lito dabbed a fresh sheen of sweat from his brow and gulped as he remained fixated on George's blade. "This captain took the small muchacho as bait because he did not believe him. And then, at night, near his boat, this captain, he sees the ojos rojo. And he believe."

James furrowed his brow. "Oho roho?"

"The red eyes. The monster, he have red eyes and you only see them right before he suck the blood."

James shuddered. He recalled the glowing red dots he had seen in the distance. He thought they were closer to understanding what they were up against now. "Go on."

Lito nodded. "The captain, he capture El Chupacabra. And he bring it back to Mexico with him to show the people the beast he got that killed his man. When ship arrive in Mexico, the people find no souls alive. All the men muerto. No blood. And El Chupacabra is missing. It jumped off the boat before they find it."

James felt his stomach twist in knots. He thought he had been scared before. Now, he wished he hadn't asked so many questions.

"El Diablo, he kill many in Mexico. Goats. Chickens. Cow. And people. Mucha gente."

George stood up. He sheathed his knife and straightened his hat. "What do you want to do with him?"

James rubbed the stubble along his chin. He figured it might be helpful to keep Lito around. Not only as help against the monster. But also to help tend the farm.

"Well, I'd say you earned something for the story."

Lito smiled wide and placed his open palm out toward James. James placed a small coin in the man's hand. Lito's smile faded.

"No mucho?"

James shrugged. "It's all I have right now. But you can come with us and we'll feed you and give you a place to sleep."

Lito began to smile again.

"In exchange for working the farm."

The smile disappeared.

"You help us work and get rid of the Chupacabra, and I'll get you more coins. I promise."

Lito bit the coin to check its weight. Satisfied it was legal tender, he pocketed the coin.

"Okay. I help you. Su casa es mi casa, eh?"

James nodded but he had no idea what he was agreeing to. He didn't understand Spanish and he was in too much of a hurry to get home to ask any more questions.

As the men climbed back in the saddle, James started to work on his explanation as to why he was bringing home a stranger, another mouth to feed.

His mother would need an answer. Now James had to sugar coat it somehow.

CHAPTER 21

Sarah controlled her displeasure for a few moments. However, it had begun to quickly get the better of her. She signaled for James to follow her to the bedroom after excusing herself from their guests.

She took a deep breath with her back to the door, waiting for James' approaching footsteps. Sarah spun quickly and pointed at the door. James understood her silent command, closing the bedroom door behind him.

"Did it ever occur to you to check with me before inviting more people to stay with us?"

James stood with his mouth agape.

"We don't know anything about this man. He could be dangerous. What if he tries to kill us all? How do you know he won't do something to Carson while we aren't paying attention? What gives you the right to make these decisions on your own?"

Sarah blurted out her frustrations with the surprise company James had brought home from town. As soon as James had introduced the man, Sarah whirled for the privacy of the other side of the house to bring her fury down on James.

"I am the man of this house, and I thought we wanted to hire help around here. His labor is cheap and we didn't have many options."

Sarah stepped toward James. "You're the man of this house? You're barely out of your teens and now you think you can run the household? I thought we were a team when it came to running the farm."

James snorted. "Were we a team when you brought George home to stay with us?"

Sarah narrowed her eyes. She disliked the tone in his voice. James insinuated that she had taken George in as something more than a guest, perhaps a lover. Her skin bristled at the gall her son could level such a claim at her.

"How dare you? George is different."

"How so?"

Sarah stuttered, "Well, for instance, we know him from Iowa. He isn't a stranger. George spent plenty of time with the three of us. Completely different from Geno."

James chuckled. "Lito. Anyway, he's more than a hired hand. He knows about the Chupacabra."

Sarah furrowed her brow. "The what?"

James explained how Lito had filled them in about the mysterious creature haunting the farm. He rattled off a litany of tales about a dog-like animal from another country that sucked blood from its victims. Her stomach twisted as her flesh prickled with goosebumps. She wasn't quite sure she could believe such tales. Yet, the similarities between the mythical creature and what they had been dealing with on the farm were too close to deny the potential reality.

"I still think you should discuss important decisions with me before going off half-cocked. We don't always have enough food for ourselves. And we certainly don't have money to pay him. Where's he going to sleep, James? You moved into Carson's room to accommodate George. We don't have a fourth room. Now what?"

James looked around Sarah's room. She held her breath, afraid he was going to suggest the strange man could stay in her room on the floor or something. She'd bring George and Carson into her room before she'd ever consider the little Mexican staying with her.

"He can sleep in the kitchen."

"On what?" Sarah swung her hands through the air. "You think he's gonna sleep sitting up in a chair. We're fresh out of beds. Plus, I don't know how comfortable I am having him stay near our food, our utensils and pans. We might wake up one morning and find everything missing." She tucked a frazzled hair behind her ear. James really hadn't thought this through and she felt too tired to figure it all out on her own.

James moved closer. He placed his hands on her shoulders and stared into her face. "I will take care of this. I'm sure I can convince George to share his room with Lito. That way, he can keep an eye on him and you don't have to worry about our food. I'll grab some of the blankets from the barn and he can sleep under them or on top of them." James sighed. "I'm sorry I acted hastily. I saw an opportunity to grab some much-needed help for our farm. And he can help us deal with that...thing out there. Lito knows all about it. I think he can really make living here a bit better."

Sarah exhaled. She had no choice but to put her faith in her son's choices. Her mind was at ease after opening up about her fears, and now she needed to take care of another man. A dirty, filthy, smelly man. Which reminded her to point it out.

"First thing you need to do is get that man into a bath. He is disgusting and I just spent the day cleaning up this place. If I find his filth coating all our things, I am going to tan your hide, mister."

James giggled. "You'd have to catch me first." He quickly ducked an open-handed slap.

Sarah bit into her lower lip. She knew she couldn't spank James anymore. There could be other ways to achieve the same end using her feminine wile. Sarah understood how one-dimensional the male brain was. She loved James to death but he was a man like all the rest.

"Go. Scrub him down and then you can get the blankets." Sarah chewed on her fingernail. "Better yet, don't put him in the bath. Lord knows what he'll leave behind in there. I don't want us sitting in his dirty water. Use the buckets and the soap flakes in the yard. If he tidies up enough, then he can use the tub next time." Sarah shuddered with disgust.

James kissed her cheek and went for the door. He paused and faced her before twisting the lever. "I think this will work. You'll see. I promised I would be the man of the house. And I won't let you down."

He left Sarah behind. Her eyes watered with affection for her boy. He had grown so much in the last few years. She knew James was a good man. He had never let her down yet.

And Sarah was sure he wouldn't in the future either. She crossed her arms and rubbed her shoulders. Life had been a struggle since she was a little girl. But family always made the hard times bearable. Family gave her something to dream about and look forward to.

Sarah loved her little family. She hoped to keep it intact as it seemed to be growing.

CHAPTER 22

Supper hit the table later than usual. Sarah had prepared a simple fare of seared squirrel legs and corn giblets. Carson grumbled under his breath about having to eat what James characterized as "tree rats." Lito dug into his meal as if he hadn't eaten in days. He chewed with his mouth open while making a humming noise.

James smiled. He watched his mother out of the corner of his eye. He knew she was particular about table manners and Lito had less than none. James winced, expecting Sarah to pounce on Lito when the man sucked the grease off the ends of his fingers with lip-smacking slurps.

Instead, Sarah bit her tongue and chose to stare down at her plate.

"Tomorrow, we'll walk the perimeter of the property so you can see what we're up against." James had warned Lito not to talk about the creature in front of Carson. However, he figured he could get away with some vague comments about their plan for the morning.

Lito continued eating without skipping a beat. He nodded in James' direction while focusing all his energy on the plate in front of him.

Carson watched Lito, fascinated with the man's ability to attack a serving of food. James bit the inside of his cheek to keep from laughing. He wondered if Carson was using Lito's exuberance as a stall tactic to keep from eating the squirrel. James remembered how Carson used to enjoy eating all kinds of meats, including squirrel. The steady diet of the tree rats must have gotten to his little friend.

James tossed a cleaned bone onto his plate. As he used his tongue to whisk strands of meat from his teeth, James realized he too had grown weary of squirrel.

"Is he living with us?" Carson hooked a thumb at Lito.

Sarah cleared her throat. "Honey, we don't talk like that in front of our guests. It's not polite."

Carson shifted his gaze to James. He whispered loud enough for the whole table to hear him. "James, is the brown guy sleeping over tonight?"

Sarah and James gasped. George chuckled into his mouthful of corn.

Lito continued to devour his meal, unabated by the commentary.

"Uh, Lito is staying for a while. He's helping us out with the chores." James checked on Lito who grunted as he drank water from his cup.

Carson leaned his head on his fist. He stared at Lito when he spoke. "Which room is Leedo sleeping in?"

"It's Lee-tow, Carson. He's gonna sleep in George's room."

George shot James a dirty look. He had been informed before supper of the arrangements and James understood George would show his displeasure every chance he got.

Carson rubbed the end of his nose. "So George is coming with us?"

"No. George and Lito will share George's room. Like you and I are sharing your room." James patted Carson's shoulder.

Carson smiled.

Lito burped and pushed forward an almost spotless plate. All that remained were bone fragments and grease. Lito had even sucked the marrow from the bones.

James waited for his mother's reaction. She gracefully dabbed at her lips with her napkin. "Mr. Lito, we don't pass gas at the dinner table. Not from our mouths and especially not from our rumps. Is that understood?"

Lito nodded. "Si, senorita. Pardon."

Sarah forced a curt smile. She waved a finger in the air as she worked to explain some more house rules. James rolled his eyes as she warned

Lito against going into any rooms without being invited in, using anything from the kitchen without permission, and the proper etiquette for bath time, specifically when it was her turn. There would be no peeking or passage in the house during her lady time.

"And we always knock before entering the outhouse. It's not polite to barge in because somebody else might be using it."

Lito nodded with a sheepish grin.

James wanted to kick the man under the table but he wasn't sure if Lito would understand his intent. He thought it would be more convenient to let it go for now rather than stir up a ruckus.

"Gracias for opening su casa to me, senorita. I will not be trouble."

George grinned at Lito. "I take care of anyone who is trouble." George snapped a leg bone in half with a loud crack.

The four of them jumped at the sudden loud noise.

Carson laughed, thinking George's show of force was funny. He picked up a squirrel leg from his own plate, still full of flesh and cold from sitting untouched. Carson worked at snapping the bones, like George, with no success. His pink tongue danced around his lips as if the effort would make the task easier.

James began to clear the plates. He left Carson's plate for last so the boy could keep playing with his food. As he moved the plates from the table to the wash basin, James attempted to wrap up the schedule for the next day.

"At first light, we'll go around the farm and check on the activity. Then we'll work on the traps and set up a line to make the most of our chances."

Lito said, "Si."

"What are we going to see?" Carson interrupted, misunderstanding Lito's agreement.

"Nothing." James tried to shoo Carson aside.

"Then why did he saided he'd see it?"

George patted James on the back. "Good luck." He strolled back to his bedroom.

"He meant 'yes'."

Carson frowned. "If you seed something then it means yes?"

James huffed. He looked to Sarah for help but she shrugged and grinned, content to let James suffer for bringing home the strange man.

"No, not that kind of see. Si, as in yes."

Carson scrunched his shoulders and placed his hands on his hips. "The ocean is a yes? That makes no sense."

Sarah chuckled.

"In Lito's tongue, si means yes." James used his hands to help explain the meaning to Carson. Instead, Carson reached into his own mouth and pulled out the end of his tongue.

"Can you thee the othen in my tongued?"

James joined Sarah in a chorus of laughter. Lito stood still and followed the action with his dark eyes.

"Never mind, Carson. Spanish is a different language and Lito speaks Spanish and English." James tossed the question to Lito for a final attempt at bridging the gap in understanding. "Any help here?"

Lito grinned and nodded profusely. "Si."

James smacked his forehead with his palm. He never imagined it would be this difficult to carry on a conversation in his own home. But, as hard as it was, James could only enjoy the moment with Carson as the boy felt around in his own mouth for what might be seen on his tongue.

CHAPTER 23

The beasts were smarter than the alpha had given them credit for. The attacks were well timed. Several waves of terror came from different directions. The pack had coordinated their efforts. The alpha respected the careful precision that must have gone into the preparations.

But would it be enough?

After dispatching the foolish pup earlier, the alpha had parked itself along the precipice of the rocky outcropping. Maintaining the high ground allowed the alpha to keep its senses focused on potential threats from all around. It also gave him a chance to nurse the wound on his hind leg. Licking the gash only made him hungrier for the next kill. And it did little to stem the flow of blood. Instead, the alpha settled on top of its hind quarters. His body weight applied ample pressure to stop the bleeding. The wound throbbed, reminding the alpha he hadn't been as smart as he thought he was.

Should've been more aware. Can't allow that to happen again.

The alpha had expected the rest. The only unknown was the timing. As dusk closed in around them, the first maneuver was made.

Two pups charged simultaneously. One approached from the right.

The other from the rear. The alpha figured the intent was to force him to pick one battle over the other so a set of fangs could rip his flesh.

The alpha reacted quickly. It swung its enormous body to the right, knocking the first animal from the top of the pile. As the creature flew backwards, the alpha opened its jaws wide to clasp the throat of the rear attacker. It snapped the mighty teeth together in a bone-crunching thud. The head tore free in a crimson splash. The alpha continued chewing on the flayed tendons caught in its gum line while the second wave moved in.

This time, three animals lurched into the fray. Again, the attackers split up, coming from several angles. The alpha lowered his left shoulder to deflect the brunt of the first dog. It changed the direction of the rush long enough for the alpha to take on the two newcomers. Razor sharp teeth nipped at the alpha's flesh. New cuts opened to loosen fresh blood. The alpha ignored the sudden flare of pain. He used his front paws to stomp one of the dogs, pinning its muzzle over a crevasse in the rocks. With a horrific howl, the alpha buried his fangs in the next dog's chest as it lunged at him. A quick toss of his head ripped out the animal's still-beating heart. The body, not understanding yet that it was dead, kept running past the alpha until the signals dimmed between the brain and the legs.

The alpha spat the juicy heart into the darkness. He dug his claws into the side of the head pinned beneath his body. Shredding flesh from the skull, the alpha used its massive weight to pound the head deeper into the crevasse, forcing the bone to collapse in on itself in order to fit not-so-neatly into the tiny space.

More dogs came. The pack had paid attention. Two or three creatures at a time hadn't been enough to subdue the monstrosity. The entire remaining group of animals thundered up the rocky mound. The alpha spun in tight circles, snapping and swatting at anything that rose above the highest stone. Claws tore through sinew. Teeth snapped bones. An enormous flurry of fur and gore lifted into the thick night. Death hung over the outcropping like an autumn fog. The battle lasted an eternity as adrenaline and sheer will were the driving forces behind the inevitable victory.

The last screams echoed across the flatlands. Only one creature still breathed.

The alpha.

His pelt had been shorn of what used to adorn his frame. The shiny coat of brown and gold existed no more. Blood-drenched and exhausted, the alpha howled at the stars above. He expelled relief as much as celebrated the win.

The way had been cleared for survival. And total domination of all living beasts within the desert range.

The humans would be next.

A true and worthy foe.

Collapsing upon the rocks, the alpha closed its eyes. It took a moment to catch its breath. The plans were already coming to fruition in its weary mind. A quick nap. Sating its belly on the flesh it had rendered to carrion. Perhaps a day or two of mending wounds and feeding on the decaying meat. And then the hunt for the future prey.

Images of the slow boy walked through its mind. Such a tasty morsel. Small enough to conquer quickly. Large enough to constitute a sizeable meal.

The alpha yawned and licked the blood from its paws. Ears darting around, the alpha listened for new dangers, content to hear silence. Even the insects had burrowed into the earth for safety. He licked his muzzle to clear away chunks of meat and coagulated blood, scent-checking the air.

All was still. Not a living organism dared to be caught in the alpha's presence after the wholesale destruction of his own pack. Even the moon had hidden from the glowing red orbs of the beast's vision.

An almost inaudible gasp crept over the piles of corpses. The alpha raised up on its haunches to find the thing that dared to draw new breath. Several yards away, one of the creatures lifted its mangled head to stare at the alpha. One eye missing, the other clouded over with brain matter, the animal lowered its head to the ground. The alpha growled, hoping to chase the ghost out of the pup so he wouldn't have to move his exhausted frame to do the job physically.

The dying wheeze signaled the beast's demise. Satisfied the army of dogs had been sent to Hell where they belonged, the alpha relaxed into the rocks. It squeezed its eyes closed, envisioning all the humans in Texas, fleeing his reign of terror. Flames licked across human dwellings, collapsing the shelters so no protection remained. Bodies strewn along the streets. Frightened women and children screaming their dying words as the alpha dragged his claws through the layers of skin, burrowing into the muscle and tendon, punching through soft organ meat like livers and kidneys and lungs before finally snagging on rib cages and shoulder bones. Arterial sprays like spring drizzle on the parched earth. The blue sky fading to a somber blackness, obliterating all rays of happiness and sunshine.

The dominion of death lay beneath the alpha's feet. A crisp wasteland as far as the eye could see.

Paradise.

CHAPTER 24

James wanted to get Lito's unadulterated input on the trap line. He knew George could be intimidating, especially for the new guest. Leaving George behind at the ranch allowed Lito to speak freely.

The pair began on the south end of the property and drove northwest along the outer reaches. Even though their closest neighbors were miles away, James had been more concerned with protecting his actual property boundaries. He knew he had to be wary of all the surrounding acreage but, in his mind, if something got within his property lines it became a real threat.

"Mucho, muchacho." Lito pointed a thick finger along the horizon. "No necessito todo."

James halted mid-step. "Would you mind speaking English so I know what the hell is going on?"

Lito chuckled. "Pardon. Sorry, senor. The land is too big to protect. Wide open spaces."

Following Lito's gesture, James knew his guest was right. The earth stretched toward the horizon in every direction. How could they possibly set up a trap line along the perimeter? They'd need thousands of traps and too much time to devise a proper boundary.

"No funnels or pinch points." Lito removed his wide-brimmed hat, fanning the morning heat from his sweaty face. "You bring El Chupacabra to you."

James felt his bowels loosen. The thought of enticing the monster to come closer wasn't even an option. How would he explain the plan to Sarah and George? His mother would yell at him. George would probably box his ears. And what about Carson? Poor little Carson was terrified of the monster. Bringing it in closer to his friend would be an unfathomable torture. James would never be able to live with himself. Especially if something horrific happened.

"No way. We can't do that."

Lito scratched his wispy mustache. "Only have two options, senor. Bring Chupacabra in or go get Chupacabra. He can be anywhere. Loco."

James fought an urge to strike Lito. His frustration was mounting and he wanted to take it out on the little man. Realistically, James understood Lito. The expanse couldn't be covered so they would have to hunt. Or be hunted. And if they chose to hunt, where would they start? What did the Chupacabra look like? What were his sleeping patterns? Travel patterns?

"If you were me, Lito, what would you do?"

The man squatted down on his haunches. He gazed east into the sun. Spitting into the dirt, Lito sighed and leveled his eyes on James.

"Quickest way to kill Chupacabra is to bring him in. He needs blood. If you have blood, he will come. And that is when you kill him."

James cracked his knuckles. The realization of luring a terrifying beast into their midst brought chills to his flesh. He had been as scared of the monster as Carson, but he had undertaken the role of "man of the house." It had been his responsibility to care for his mother and Carson. Although George brought brawn and toughness, James had agreed to the task (even bragged about it) of being the one to see to their safety and well-being.

He'd never be able to reveal his plan to Sarah and Carson.

Could he even get away with this deception?

After surviving the previous horrors that plagued them, would he be capable of leading them into another battle with death? The reason they had come to Texas was to escape the evils of the world. To find peace. To live an ordinary life of farming and husbandry.

Instead, they had run into the waiting jaws of something far more formidable than they had encountered previously.

"If I decide to do this, you have to promise me you will not reveal the plan to my mother or Carson." James poked a finger into Lito's chest. "Not even George. I'll handle him."

Lito held up his hands and chuckled. "I won't tell him. I no like him. He wants to hurt me."

James nodded. "George is more bark than bite. But you're better off staying away from him. He is not a fan of people of color. In fact, he doesn't trust white folks either."

They started to make their way back toward the ranch. The conversation danced from lures to how big a trap they should build to the kill shot. Lito explained that not many have lived to tell the tale of El Chupacabra. Those who encountered the beast usually perished. Legends and embellished campfire stories remained to fill in the gaps. He opened up about the one time he had witnessed the monster in his village in Mexico. It had fed on the animals and children. Then it had attacked the elder's wife but couldn't finish the job of sucking her dry of blood because a group of men had interrupted its feast. El Chupacabra devoured the men and disappeared into the night before a party of villagers charged onto the scene. The elder's wife succumbed to her injuries later that night. And little Lito had remained silent about the details of that horrific night. He had stayed in his hiding spot for several days, too traumatized by what he had witnessed to come out. And too afraid the monster knew he had watched; he feared it would return to take his soul for his sins.

"I left Mexico because I was afraid of El Chupacabra. And now he is here like I am. Perhaps it is my destiny to give El Diablo my blood for seeing what he did. And not helping my fellow villagers."

James began to feel sorry for Lito. The man appeared to be resigned to dying at the fangs of the beast. Maybe he could save Lito from his despair. And maybe Lito could conquer his inner demons from the past. Together they could do what no others had been able to. Defeat the devil.

He admonished himself for once again believing he could save the world from evil. James shook his head in resignation. Some habits died hard and fighting the ills of the earth had been everything James had dreamed about. He had tried to run from his calling but Lito had summed it up perfectly.

Destiny.

James had never given much thought to the word and the meaning as it pertained to his own life. Yet, it made a lot of sense. James had it in his blood. His father had defeated bad men across the country. And James had followed in his father's footsteps. Willingly and sometimes unknowingly.

This would be one of those times. James smiled. He felt right for the first time since they had left Dodge.

CHAPTER 25

Sarah had found the gold chain in the pocket of Carson's dungarees. She'd risen early to take care of wash and bumped into James and Lito. They told her they were going to walk the property so Lito knew what he needed to work on to earn his keep. As she unscrambled the clothes to run them through the sudsy water, she felt something inside Carson's pocket. At first, Sarah figured the boy had left a stick or some other detritus from the landscape in his jeans. He would bring home all kinds of trinkets and junk he found on his adventures around the farm.

Gold was not something she would have imagined finding.

She held the object aloft, taking in the glint of metal where it peeked through grime and dirt. A Christian cross. Sarah's thoughts wandered to places Carson might have encountered such a treasure. Her stomach sunk at the thought of Carson stealing the gold chain from their trip into town. George had jokingly claimed he had caught Carson stealing from the store. But what if the boy HAD really lifted someone's precious possession?

He's not capable of such a thing.

Sarah quickly dismissed her little boy's theft. Carson didn't have a mean bone in his body. And he had never stolen anything when they had lived in the brothels where money and jewels were rampant. So why would he start now, in Texas of all places?

Deciding to get to the bottom of the mystery, Sarah woke Carson. She held the necklace in front of his sleepy eyes which shot wide with horror at her discovery. Sarah questioned where Carson had come across the gold. He slumped his shoulders and admitted finding it along the rocky outcropping. He told her it had shined in the sunlight and drawn him to its location. Carson confided the gold chain had been on the cross of a grave site.

Her flesh bristled.

While it was common practice for people to bury their dead on their own land, Sarah couldn't help but get chills at the thought of a grave marker on their property. It was something she had never had to consider as they had lived above saloons for many years, with no land to call their own.

Sarah asked Carson to get dressed and take her to the place he had discovered. Begrudgingly, Carson threw on his clothes and led Sarah to the spot which had been further away from the ranch than Sarah felt comfortable with. She pushed away visions of Carson traveling that far from the house, unsupervised and alone. Sarah made a mental note to tell James so they could both keep a closer eye on Carson's whereabouts.

As they neared the grave site, Sarah glanced around and wondered why the body would be buried so far from the home. Folks would not wish to forget their loved ones. They would bury the dead in the yard so they could tend to the site and visit the deceased. It seemed unlikely to keep the grave at such a distance, unless the family wanted to make a pilgrimage of sorts each time they visited.

Drummond.

The name carved into the sticks was difficult to discern. Sarah rubbed the dust from the grooves to be sure it was indeed Drummond. The cross was very primitive and showed considerable wear from time. It leaned eastward a bit.

Carson brought Sarah a threadbare hat which he had found at the location that same day. He held the hat up to her face so she could see the sweat stains along the inside of the brim. The hat resembled more of a farmer's style rather than that of a cowpoke. It was designed to shade the eyes and keep the sun off the neck of the owner. A cowpoke's hat would be built more for style, matching the personality of the hired hand.

"When did you find these things?"

Carson shrugged. "I was playinged in the yard and I seed it from the rocks." Carson pointed to the outcropping a good fifty yards away.

"This isn't quite the yard, young man. You know you aren't supposed to wander off without James. What if you fall and break your leg or get lost? How will we be able to help you if we don't know where you are?"

Carson kicked at the dirt along his boots. Sarah knew when Carson was upset. He would keep his head down and avoid eye contact. She didn't want to start him off for the day with a chastising. Sarah rubbed the back of his neck.

"I'm not mad. I just worry about you, sweetie. I love you and I don't want you to get hurt."

Carson lightened and smiled at her. Sarah smiled in return.

"Does James know?"

"I forgotted to tell him."

Sarah placed her hands together as if she were praying. "Well, let's keep this our little secret for now, okay? James has a lot on his mind and I don't want him to think about this grave too."

Carson nodded enthusiastically. "Oh boy. A secret. No James."

He did a little dance, kicking up clouds of dust. Sarah giggled and shooed Carson back toward the farm. As he sprinted toward the house, Sarah paused to take another look at the cross. The mystery of its origin and choice of location tugged at the back of her mind. She hoped it was the only one of its kind on the property. Sarah would talk to George and see if he had noticed any markers in his hunt for the thing that haunted them at night. She'd ask George to keep his eyes open for similar tombs in his travels around the farm.

In the meantime, Sarah would try to figure out the meaning behind such an odd discovery.

Could it have anything to do with the creature that disturbed them? If so, how long has the monster been stalking the grounds? Could the evil be something ancient that had withstood the hardships of the desert, and outlasted several generations of existence in this remote part of Texas?

Sarah lifted her skirt hem to catch up with Carson. She hadn't run in a long time but the exertion shook her from her deep fears. The wind felt cool as it ruffled through her hair. She called out to Carson that she was going to get him, scaring a frightful squeak out of him. She watched Carson kick into another gear as the thought of something hunting him from behind motivated his legs to churn faster.

The sight of his speed relieved her. She hoped Carson wouldn't need to rely on his fast little legs to save his life someday.

CHAPTER 26

George strode directly at James. He wore the expression of an angry rattlesnake. James had to think fast, conjuring a lie to fend off a confrontation. He knew he had to devise a plan behind everyone's back but he had anticipated having a bit more time to develop it.

"Where'd you go?" George stepped inside James' personal space. Rather than giving into the larger man, James decided to show no weakness. He remained stoic and maintained direct eye contact with George.

"I took Lito around. Showed him the farm."

George spat a wad of juice on James' boots. He ignored the attempt to elicit a physical response.

"No reason to get your dander up. We just took a walk. Ain't that right, Lito?" James never took his eyes from George's.

"Si."

George chewed the wad of leaf in his mouth. He used his tongue to shift the mush from one cheek to the other. "Mmhm."

James stepped to the right, preferring not to step backwards but still giving himself room to breathe. "That's right. I'm not gonna do anything without you, George. I need your help to get the Screeper."

The admission appeared to appease George. The man backed down.

"What is Screeper?" Lito tapped James' shoulder.

James chuckled. "Never mind. It's a nickname we have for the..."

Carson came charging from the porch. He shouted for James, interrupting his answer. Carson jumped up into James' arms. He carried on about how excited he was for James to come home.

"I knowed something but you don't."

James knitted his eyebrows. Before he could question what Carson meant, Sarah moved closer.

"Haha, Carson is so funny. What are we going to work on first, boys? The chicken coop needs cleaning. The animals must be fed. I've got dirty laundry working right now. And we still need to get a new pen built for the horses." She rubbed her hands together as if she were excitedly awaiting the volunteers to step forward.

James frowned. "Gosh, we just got back. Don't we get time to have breakfast and coffee?"

Sarah shook her head. "Nope. You should've thought of that before you went off earlier. The day is getting old and we're falling behind on our work."

George laughed at James getting scolded. He shot the big man a dirty look and listened to Lito snickering next to him.

"Fine. Lito will help me set up the horse pen. Carson will feed the animals. And George," James grinned at his old friend, "Will clean out the chicken coop."

James grabbed Lito's arm, tugging him in the direction of the new pen to escape George's lamentation at getting assigned the nasty work. To his surprise, James glanced over his shoulder as George sauntered toward the chickens without a word. Partly relieved and partly shocked, James transferred his thoughts to the horse pen. It would require some hard manual labor to drive the posts into the arid ground. Then they'd need to carry the over-sized lumber supports and notch them into the posts. George's stature was more suited to such a task but James was sick of feeding the animals. And he desperately wanted to retaliate against George for spitting on his boots. It was far easier to dispatch George to poop duty than to challenge the man to a fight.

As they struggled to pound down the posts, Lito and James debated the trap location and the type of bait to use. James had argued to kill some coyotes and string up the carcasses near the wood line he and George had scouted. Lito disagreed vehemently. He countered the Chupacabra desired fresh blood. The monster would not come running for something that was already dead. It would take live bait to draw it in. He also recommended steering clear of the woods.

"Too dangerous, mi amigo. With trees, you can't see what might be hiding. Best to keep to the open so you can watch your surroundings."

"But if we are out in the open, then the Chupacabra will see us. Won't he be discouraged from coming closer? He won't knowingly walk right into a trap."

Lito rested on the post hole digger. He brushed the sweat from his brow with his sleeve. "El Chupacabra, he very smart. But he is still an animal. The need for food will take over if he weighs his chances and the probabilidades is good."

James considered the idea. Stringing up live meat for the monster. Out in the open. They'd have to be far enough away to protect themselves but close enough to get a kill shot on the monster. They'd have one chance only. James understood that if they failed the Chupacabra would learn of their intent and it would steer clear of such a trap in the future.

It had to work the first time.

The only time.

"I'll have to think about this. I'm not sure how we can pull it off without scaring him off."

Lito chuckled. "You no scare him off. El Chupacabra afraid of nothing. You'll see."

James huffed. It felt as if his plan to get rid of the creature got further away from him each time he felt better about it. The beast had proven to be an enigma, as much in reality as in planning.

"You said he is a goat sucker but I'm not sparing one of my kids for him. I want to use something from my trap line."

"No bueno. El Diablo can have rabbits and squirrels any time he wants. He wants what he can't have. Real blood from a creature he dreams about. Something more than he find out there." Lito nodded over his shoulder at the desert.

James lost his patience. He had grown weary of Lito's obtuse hints. "And what is that, Lito? I'm tired of your games. Be straight for once."

Lito's grin faded. His toothless lips spread for a dry tongue to clear away the grit lining his mouth. "Man."

James threw down his hatchet. "Don't give me this man crap. What kind of meat does it want? Tell me what I need to tease it with so I can kill this damned thing." He grabbed Lito's shirt collars and shook the chubby man in his fist.

Lito glared into James' face. He swallowed a lump and whispered.

"Man. El Chupacabra desires the blood of man, chico."

James froze. Never in his wildest nightmares had he considered using his family or friends, not even himself, to lure the devil into range. Somehow, the truth of the statement drove a stake through his heart. James knew Lito was right.

He wished it wouldn't be the case.

James released Lito from his grasp. He stepped back and stared into the light blue heavens above. James had never been a very religious soul. In this moment, he searched for God's help in the skies above.

CHAPTER 27

George refused to give in. He'd swallow his pride. For the moment. Later, James would get what was coming to him. It was too important for him to remain in Sarah's good graces. His goal of finding her and making her his woman was the whole reason George had traveled in search of them. James wouldn't undo it for him.

He scraped chicken crap off the edges of the wood. The space was narrow and difficult for him to navigate. Several birds clucked and shambled beneath his legs to escape the disturbance. A few others were steadfast, pecking at his hands, and one cheeky chicken took a peck at his face. George backhanded the bird into another bin. It whined and caterwauled as it hustled away. George spat a plume of tobacco in the bird's tracks, nearly coating the bird in dark saliva.

George chuckled to himself.

The sound of Carson's howls shook George from his job. He poked his head through a small window in the back of the coop. Carson ran away from the huge pig and a garrison of smaller animals. George realized the others were too far away to respond to Carson's cries. He rolled his eyes and left the coop to aid the little boy.

George stepped through the gate as Carson came his way. The boy hid behind George's long legs. He buried his face into George's rump.

George clapped his hands together which stopped all the animals in their tracks. Except for the large pig. It lumbered forward and shoved its snout into George's crotch. His knees buckled as the force sent waves of pain from his groin to his brain. Before dropping to the mud, George punched the large pig in the side. It ran away grunting and squawking.

The little animals followed suit.

George rubbed his nuts and winced at the sky. It had been a while since he had taken a shot to the jewels. He couldn't say he missed the feeling.

Carson stepped in front of him. "Are you hurted?"

George spat leaf juice. "You can say that, kid."

Sarah waved over to them. George waved back at her and forced a smile. He muttered under his breath how convenient it was that she saw Carson now and not before he had entered the pen and got his hide kicked.

Carson went into a flurry of words about how Tina had tried to eat the food right from his hand and he had run away. She had chased him to get the food in his fist. George sneered. "You should probably drop the feed then."

He began to head back for the coop when Carson stopped him dead in his tracks.

"I knowed a secret. James don't." Carson grinned like he was up to no good. George became instantly intrigued. He wondered if Carson would spill the beans that Sarah was in love with him and was so glad he had arrived on her doorstep. Once he knew her intentions were the same, George would quit beating around the bush and come right out with his proposal. He had thought about it for a long time and George was positive that Sarah was the woman for him. She had been the only one who hadn't scoffed at him or whisked him away as undesirable. The fact that she chastened him to bathe himself left him to believe she cared for him in a way nobody else ever had.

Not even his momma.

"What's the secret, squirt?" George knelt to get to Carson's level. The big reveal hung in the air like an anvil ready to drop into a lake with a huge splash.

"There's a grave here on the perpiddy."

George grunted.

"A grave?" His eyes glanced over Carson's shoulders to watch Sarah bend over the wash. "So what."

Carson threw his hands on his hips. "It hadded gold and a cross and whiskey. Oh, and a hat too." He nodded like he was the teacher at the front of the classroom confirming a historical fact.

George rose to his feet. He felt disappointed. His fantasy of learning Sarah's feelings for him had been much better than Carson's little story.

"Gold, huh? How much gold?"

Carson shrugged. "I finded a necklace with a gold cross. I tried to hide it but Sarah finded it in my pants. She made me showed her the grave. And she tolded me to keep a secret so James wouldn't get sore."

George wondered why Sarah would keep something so trivial from James. Unless it were something more important than Carson understood. Perhaps it had lots of gold and Sarah wanted to keep the wealth to herself. It didn't seem feasible with all he knew about Sarah. More likely she wanted to keep the gold from James before he went and spent it all on farm hands and plows and such. James was still green enough to run through town with a stack of money in his hands for every con man and salesman in sight to swarm him.

He'd have to get to the bottom of it.

"Can you show me where the grave is, Carson? I'd like to look it over."

The boy shook his head. "I dunno. She might get real sore at me for showing you." Carson whispered behind his hand. "I'm not supposed to tell anybody the secret."

George stifled a laugh. "Oh, I get it. I can keep the secret too. Just you and me, buddy, right?"

Carson nodded and grinned.

"But just supposing somebody who knew the secret wanted to know where it was to keep James from seeing it. Then where would the person with the secret steer James away from?"

Carson ran to the fence. He climbed up and pointed toward the plains. "Over there. It's small and dirty but the sun shined on the whiskey bottle so you can seed it."

George glared along the line where Carson had pointed. He picked out a few markers he could count on to guide him in the direction once he had a chance to scope out the location for himself.

"Our secret." George zipped his lip and Carson imitated him. "Anything else Sarah doesn't want James to know?"

Carson whispered behind his hand again. "There might be more graves on the perpiddy and she wants to find them before James does."

George scratched his stubble. One grave wasn't a big deal. More graves might not amount to much either. It was customary to bury family members on the land. However, George found it perplexing the grave marker had been so far away from the ranch.

Something about that made him curious.

George would look into the matter on his own.

And he would use it to find out what Sarah was trying to hide.

CHAPTER 28

Sarah finished the laundry. She took a few moments to supervise the rest of the crew on their progress. George had cleaned up the chicken coop better than any of them had in the past. He had joined James and Lito on the horse pen. Sarah was happy the three of them worked together so the task would be completed sooner. George's size and power would go a long way toward the back-breaking work to drive the posts and secure the beams.

Carson played in the yard. He hummed songs and chased a lizard across the ground.

With everyone preoccupied, Sarah hurried to make a quick search of the land. She wanted to find out of there were any other undiscovered grave sites around the farm. The one Carson had showed her had weighed on her mind. Sarah knew James would find out eventually. She figured it would probably behoove her to reveal the discovery sooner rather than later so they can make sense of it.

Yet, she worried what it would do to James. He had taken on too much with the purchase of the farm and his promise to care for the family. Adding George as another mouth to feed and bringing Lito to the homestead only exacerbated the pressure.

Sarah sneaked periodic glances over her shoulder to ensure she could get away with her secret search. If the men found her out, she figured she could lie and say she was chasing a bunny around for dinner. Hopefully, James wouldn't yell at her to just check the trap lines instead.

She had forgotten about Carson.

He danced and sang aloud as he came toward her.

Dammit!

Sarah looked past Carson. The men continued to work, unaware of Carson's distraction. She sighed and rubbed her palms along her skirt.

Boys will be boys.

"I'm finding treasure." Carson shielded his eyes from the sun as he spoke to Sarah.

"How exciting." Sarah decided to take advantage of Carson's presence. He could help her scout and act as an excuse should the men take an interest in their activities. "I am too. Wanna help me find buried treasure?"

"Oh boy!"

Sarah instructed Carson to scour the ground for more gold chains or anything else that might be out of place. She had him flank her right so she could keep a protective eye on him while simultaneously covering more yard. Sarah had hardly finished speaking when Carson took off on his quest. She laughed and got to work herself.

They covered the entire western side of the property without incident. Nothing appeared strange. No trinkets or lost items from a bygone era. Sarah pointed Carson north. The terrain grew increasingly rockier as the team headed northeast. She knew the grave site they had found was ahead and to the right, on the way to the rocky outcropping. But Sarah was determined to clear the way to that pile of stones, hoping she wouldn't find more of what she feared.

Two hours later, Sarah had grown tired. Carson had climbed the rocky hill and sat down. He used a stick he had picked up to scratch along the stony surface. Sarah exhaled, glad for the short respite. She took a seat on the rocks, choosing not to climb as high as Carson had gone. The afternoon breeze loosened her long dark hair from its bun. Wisps tickled her cheeks as they shifted along her visage in the wind. She closed her eyes for a few minutes, enjoying the sun's warmth on her face, listening to the contentedness of Carson's whimsical playing.

A shadow drifted across her face, blotting out the sunlight.

Sarah opened her eyes and gasped.

The afternoon sun was eclipsed by the enormous shadow of a man. George.

He stood over her with his arms folded across his chest.

"You startled me."

George smirked. "In a good way?"

Sarah laughed. "If you had surprised me, it would've been in a good way. I suppose startling someone is the opposite."

George sat next to Sarah on the bottom of the rock pile. She reminded herself to teach him to ask if he could sit next to a lady in the future. George's manners still required a woman's touch. She let it go for the time being, happy to have him nearby.

"You both wandered far off." George pursed his lips to spit tobacco but seemed to think better of it. He stopped himself and swallowed. Sarah choked back some bile that threatened to creep up her throat.

"Did James send you to check on me? Or did you come of your own accord?"

"Does it matter?" George stretched his legs and leaned back along the rocks.

"You tell me." Sarah tried to remember the last time she had enjoyed an entreating flirtation. It had been quite some time. She had faked flirtations with customers, but the last time she had truly flirted and enjoyed it had been when she met James' father, Wyatt Earp. He had been a real man she could have fallen in love with.

George filled her in on the progress of the horse pen. He warned Sarah not to trust the Mexican. He had a distrustful feeling about the man James had brought home. But he agreed the man's labor was helpful. After a short break in the conversation where they both sat in silence, listening to Carson playing above them, George changed the line of discussion.

"Find any more grave sites?"

Sarah twisted her frame to immediately stare at George.

"What are you talking about?"

George smirked. "I know about the cross and the grave."

Sarah shot a disappointed look in Carson's direction. However, the boy played without realizing he had been in her crosshairs.

"It's nothing to fret over. Families bury their dead nearby all the time." She shrugged her shoulders non-challantly.

"Hm. I thought it was strange because the grave is so far away from the ranch. Almost, like they was trying to hide it for some reason."

Sarah was impressed with George's deduction. She had always considered him a big, strong ruffian. Not particularly stupid. But not intelligent enough to pick up on subtleties. It suddenly irked her a bit more because he was probably smart enough to know his manners then. Yet, he chose to act like an uncouth gorilla.

Sarah would store that away for future use as well.

"Perhaps the home had been closer and it was moved for a reason."

George spat. "Easier to move a grave than a whole house, wouldn't you reckon?"

Sarah grimaced at him. "MUST you spit that horrendous filth in my presence? Seriously."

George smiled wide, tobacco leaves wedged in between his front teeth.

She shielded her laugh with her hand. "You are incorrigible."

They laughed hard as George nodded in agreement. He placed a large hand upon her knee.

Sarah trembled with delight.

CHAPTER 29

After supper, James and Lito stepped onto the porch. Darkness had closed in like a wool blanket around a newborn. Except there had been far less comfort in the air. James strained his ears for approaching danger. His eyes scanned the yard, intent on locating the tell-tale red orbs lying in wait.

Lito tried to comfort James by explaining how El Chupacabra would seek to pick them off, one by one, before he would attack an entire household of people.

"I'm not sure I trust something I can't see." James rotated the barrel of his pistol, satisfied with the clicking sound as each round rolled past the hammer. He aimed the gun at a distant fence post, barely visible in the dusk, and sighted the barrel at the wood.

"Don't hurt yourself, kid."

James lowered the gun while George pulled up a chair alongside him.

"Haha, very funny."

George wedged an enormous wad of tobacco leaf in his jawline. He snickered at James.

"Do I have to separate you two? Always at each other's throats every time I turn around." Sarah stuck her head out the door. Carson slipped under her arm and hurried to a stool in the corner of the porch. Sarah closed the door and joined the men for a bit of fresh air.

"He started it." James bit his lower lip as soon as the words passed his teeth. He sounded like a child, whining to his momma. James felt the blush color his cheeks for tattling.

"Aww, poor baby. Want me to warm you some milk?" Sarah patted James' shoulder. George and Carson giggled.

"I would like some milk, senorita." Lito raised a hand to summon his request.

Sarah ignored Lito and took a seat in a slightly off-kilter rocking chair.

"We don't have milk, Lito." James admonished his guest. "She was teasing me."

Lito blinked uncomprehending of the joke.

"Forget it." James waved his hand. "Think we'll have a visit tonight?"

Carson, who had been content to sit along the porch railing, changed his mind as soon as there was mention of the monster. He dragged his stool away from the edge and tucked it behind George's chair. In his new location, Carson would be surrounded by James and George with the house behind his back.

James chastised himself for scaring Carson. He had only meant to change the conversation from everyone thinking he was a baby to something else. His awkward transition had frightened his little pal.

"Carson, have you shown Lito how to play poker yet?"

"Uh-uh." Carson shook his head.

Lito sneered. "I no like to take money from children."

James chuckled. "We don't play for money, Lito. Just for fun."

"Well, Carson has fun. James just loses." Sarah threw in her two cents.

Laughter filled the porch once again.

As he was about to go inside, pouting like a child, James noticed the red dots in the distance.

"Look!" He pointed so the others would follow his line.

Carson squealed and ran into the house. Sarah gasped. She clutched her face between her hands. "I hope to God it stays away. I better go sit with Carson." She went to the door. "James, what are we going to do tonight?"

He felt all eyes on him. His plan had to hold muster or he'd risk failing his family. "I will keep lookout tonight. And then George can do it tomorrow."

"Smarter to break it into shorter shifts. You ever stay up all night before?" George asked the question without taking his eyes from the red orbs.

James considered George's suggestion. It made sense. He wished he had thought it out before blurting his response. Better to cover himself quickly.

"Good idea. I'll take first shift. Then George. And if we need it, Lito can finish off the night into the morning."

George elbowed James. "He ain't got no weapon. You feel comfortable leaving him with your gun? I don't"

James winced at George's blatant disregard for Lito's feelings. Although, James had initially thought about some form of torture to get info out of Lito when they had brought him home. And now he cared for the man's feelings? James clenched his fist in his lap to toughen himself up. He felt as if he had been going soft since he had "quit" the hero business.

"No. Me neither. Not yet." James acknowledged Lito directly. "No offense, but we just met you."

Lito held up his hands to show the comments bounced off him.

"So then what? Back to you and me only?" George spat a plume of juice which disappeared the moment it left his lips.

"No. Lito can stand guard and shout if it makes a move. Then you and I can come running. You okay with that, Lito?"

Lito nodded. "Si, just hurry when I scream."

In all the discussion, James had taken his eyes off the red orbs. He had lost them now. Searching along the land, James slapped his knee in disgust.

"Lost them."

George pointed. "I seen them go that way. They blinked and then moved off."

Even with the helpful directions, James knew it wouldn't matter where the beast was out there. It had the advantage of the night. And the quarry was stationary. He worried the creature would spring into action once there was one individual alone on the porch. Seeing how he had volunteered himself first, his stomach fluttered with butterflies.

"Best get some rest now. I'll come tap you when it's your time."

George nodded and went into the house. Lito rose in front of James.

"Senor, por favor, El Chupacabra is evil. You must be mucho careful." He offered his hand. James shook Lito's thick fist. He wished his guest a good night and then returned his attention to the black ink of the desert night.

His eyes played tricks on him. From his peripheral vision, James caught shadows darting along the edges of the porch. He sat up straight, pinning his body so that he wouldn't move a muscle. James needed to focus every bit of his sight and hearing on the vast fields. He squeezed the pistol handle in his fist, feeling the moisture of his nervous sweat dampen the weapon. It was going to be a long night, but James felt most comfortable with his own abilities to stand watch. George was handier in a fight, James knew, and he'd rather put the big man against any threat.

Tonight, James needed to earn the respect of his family. The time for boasting and talking about protecting them was over.

Now he had to show them.

CHAPTER 30

The first watch passed without much incident. Red eyes hadn't been spotted a second time. However, the night had been filled with growls and distant screams. The sounds brought chills to his skin, forcing his body to stay alert, watching for an ambush.

It helped that the air had cooled down. The crisp, cold night kept James shivering and moving. He tapped his foot or rubbed his arms to keep himself warm, forcing the blood to his extremities.

Once his three hours were up, James went inside to rouse George. It took a few pokes to wake the large man who had fallen into deep slumber. George grumbled when he found James hovering over his bed. He rolled over so his feet slipped into his boots, pushing James aside to clear a path to the door. James followed George to the porch to make sure he didn't go right back to sleep. George stared at James long enough to make him feel uncomfortable. At that point, James knew George was angry and would stay on guard with a full-on attitude.

It made James feel safer knowing George was angry.

James glanced in his mother's room to check on her and Carson. The boy was tucked into the corner along the wall. Sarah slept right up against Carson with her arm draped over his side. The sound of soft breathing signaled James that they were getting rest. He gently closed the bedroom door and crawled into Carson's bed. Glad to close his eyes and rest his weary body, James still felt out of sorts. Carson's bed was a bit small and stiff. But still better than sitting on the porch all night.

His mind raced through all that had happened in recent days. George. Lito. The Screeper. Life had been so much simpler a short while ago. And now they were right in the middle of another battle with something evil. Something unnatural.

James rolled over, pulling the thin blanket over his hip and legs. The bed was just as uncomfortable on his side as it was on his back. He sighed at the wall.

Lito had suggested they use a live human being to lure the monster in. Who would it be? James couldn't endanger his family. George could probably fight the creature and win. But James wouldn't make his friend do what he wasn't willing to do himself.

It had to be James.

What if the Chupacabra killed him though? Who would avenge his death? What would happen to the farm? How would his mother survive without his help? Who would look after Carson? It frustrated James to think about all the scenarios where he lost his life and the family had to go on without him.

And what if James won? Were there more Chupacabras out there? Would they smell the death and come to bring revenge upon James and his family? What if you couldn't kill the Chupacabra? From the stories he had heard, it sounded like this creature has survived centuries of mankind, and on more than one continent. Did James really feel like he could do what many men had failed to do before him?

James rolled onto his back again. He stared at the ceiling. Sleep and comfort evaded him. He tried to imagine how he could entice the monster to come for him. James pictured himself standing in the desert heat, roped to a cottonwood tree, waiting for the beast to come in close. He could smell its dank breath, the jaws drooling soupy strands of saliva as it impatiently approached its next meal. James waited until it got closer...closer...closer...

He pulled his gun from behind his waistband and fired directly into the Chupacabra's face.

It wouldn't work.

James groaned. He kicked the blanket off his legs, feeling perspiration boil under the layers of his skin.

The thing won't hunt him in the daylight.

It would have to be night.

And the stakes would be much higher.

James would be blind in the dark. He was a creature of sunlight.

El Chupacabra would be dangerous at night. It was a killing machine, built to rely on its night vision and strong sense of smell. The beast would be deft at tracking and killing its prey in the awful darkness.

James would be blind in the dark.

A distant screech lifted the hair on his arms. James scrambled over to the window. He peered into the inky expanse. The sound of George shifting his weight on the porch as he maneuvered brought wooden creeks to the window frame. James watched from Carson's window, content to forgo sleep for the night. He felt better keeping George company, of course, without George knowing it.

He weighed some different options. Perhaps he could use Lito to attract the beast. Lito wasn't family. James had grown to like the man but he didn't know him well enough to care whether he lived or died. He shook his head in disgust. He couldn't do that to Lito either. Maybe he could bring some hired guns in from town to fight the monster. But how would that work? Would he just walk into town and ask for people to come kill a monster? They would think he was crazy, and he would have difficulty getting his way with anything in town in the future. Or, if the townsfolk believed him, it could go one of two ways. The gun-crazy hunters would swarm to his ranch and tear everything up trying to find the beast. Or, the troublesome folks would target James and the ranch, thinking it would be easy pickings to take advantage of a crazy young man and his lonely family.

Either scenario made James nervous.

No, he reasoned, he'd have to do it on his own. Anything else wouldn't be right.

In the dark.

Alone.

James felt his tongue dry up with the thought of being on his own in the wilds with whatever type of animal could make the blood-curdling sounds he heard every night. His mind worked over how to make the gun an advantage when he couldn't see clearly enough for a shot. The gun might not be the weapon of choice. He might need to use something more reliable. Something he could feel and manipulate without requiring daylight for optimal accuracy.

Like a knife blade.

Another screech filled the air.

James rubbed his chin.

It would have to be one hell of a knife blade to stand up to the thing that could make noises like that.

He rested his head along the windowsill, praying a better idea would come to him.

Soon.

CHAPTER 31

Sarah woke before dawn. She slipped away from Carson's warm embrace, leaving him curled up in the blanket on her bed. Tiptoeing as quietly as she could, Sarah pulled the bedroom door shut after her.

James sat in the dark on Carson's bed. He glanced up at Sarah as she entered the room.

"Have you slept?" Sarah yawned through her palm.

"Not really." James stood and went to the window. He sighed as he gazed into the night. "I felt better helping out."

Sarah rubbed James' shoulder. She felt the tension in his muscles. Sarah massaged his neck for a moment and then patted his lower back. James still carried the weight of the world around with him, she thought. He'd probably never change. James had been a caring and worrisome child, and the traits had followed him into his young adulthood.

Looking through the window to the porch, Sarah noticed the shape of the sentry on duty. It was smaller than she had expected.

"Is that Lito out there?"

James mumbled a soft, "Hm-hm."

Sarah wondered how long she and Carson had been asleep. If James and George had served their shifts already, it had to be after three in the morning.

"The screams stopped while George was on watch. Lasted almost to the end of his shift. It's been quiet since."

Lito rocked his chair gently, a slight creaking noise drifted to the window on the forward motion. Sarah thought it was a bit irresponsible of Lito to make even the tiniest of noises as anything could signal the monster to come investigate the disturbance. Irresponsibility awakened her own guilt about hiding the grave site Carson had discovered.

James returned to the bed. He slumped down, resting his head in his hands. Sarah could sense his exhaustion. James had been working hard without a break for quite some time. She feared he would fall apart before they could rid themselves of their pest problem or make the decision to move to another place, avoiding all the stress of their current home.

"Lito said it needs blood. Human blood."

Sarah gasped. "How would he know? He just got here."

"This...thing is from Mexico or wherever. He told us stories of how it has killed men around the world. Lots of men. It is fierce. And it feeds on man."

She sat next to James, giving his knee a gentle squeeze. "Sweetie, do you really believe him? He could've lied so you would take him in, thinking you needed him."

"I do need him. We need as many hands as we can get. It won't be easy to hunt this creature in the dark."

"In the dark?" Sarah brushed the hair on the side of James' head. "Why not go after it during daylight? I thought you were going to build a trap so we wouldn't have to hunt."

James sighed. He rubbed his thighs and rose, pacing the room. "The trap isn't really a trap. It's more like bait."

Sarah grimaced at the sound of his voice. Sarah knew when James lied or tried to hide the truth. Right now, she had him to dead to rights. "There is something you aren't telling me." She approached James, squaring off in front of him.

"I have to bait the Chupacabra in with human meat. Blood. But it only eats living flesh."

"James, I don't like where this is going. You're going to sacrifice Lito's life? How could you do that to an innocent man?"

James cut her off. "Not Lito. Me. I'm going to use myself to lure it close so we can kill it."

Sarah raised her voice. "Over my dead body."

James waved his hands for her to lower her voice. She realized she might wake up George or startle Carson from his dreams.

"Are you crazy? What happens if it kills you?" As soon as she said the words, the image of the grave site passed in her mind's eye.

"I won't let it kill me." James ran a hand through his hair, circling away from Sarah's scrutiny.

"James, there's something you should know."

He turned to face her. Sarah struggled to look him in the face. She felt guilty for keeping the secret from him.

"Carson showed me something. I didn't want to tell you because you're overburdened already." She wringed her hands, searching for the softest way to reveal the discovery. "Carson found a grave on the property. Out by the rocks."

James shrugged. "So?"

"So, maybe it is the grave of somebody the Chupacabra got."

"I don't think so. The previous owner disappeared. Ran off or something. His family would've told me if the monster had killed him."

Sarah snorted. "Are you sure of that? You don't think they would've brushed that under the rug if it made it easier to sell the farm? Why do you think it was so cheap?"

James weighed her questions while scratching his arm. "It was cheap because they needed the money so they could move away. The farm was too much for them without him."

"And it had nothing to do with a young rube from out of town? Someone who they could unload this dangerous place on? Someone who had no idea what had really happened here in the past?"

James slammed a fist into his palm. "You think I'm stupid? Is that it?"

Sarah rushed to James. She squeezed his face in between her hands. "No, honey. I think you are too innocent for your own good sometimes. That's all. And those people took advantage of you. It happens often, folks sinning against their fellow man."

James tore her hands away. He squatted in front of the window, staring at the coming morning. "I'll check it out at daylight. What else didn't you tell me?"

She told James about the hat and the whiskey bottle. Sarah explained how Carson had brought home a gold necklace with a Christian cross on the end of it. Real gold. And she mentioned there was a name carved into the make-shift grave marker.

"Name. What name?"

Sarah tapped her chin, trying to remember the name. "Desmond. Diamond. I think."

He spun on his heels. Sarah reacted with a start at how quickly James had reacted to the names. She felt her heart pounding in her chest.

"Could it be Drummond?"

Sarah's eyes went wide. "Yes. I think that was it. Drummond." She gingerly moved toward James. "What is it, James?"

"Drummond was the name of the man who went missing. The previous owner of this farm." James plopped himself on Carson's bed. He shook his head, staring at the floor.

Sarah understood her fears had been realized.

And now it was too late to get their money back.

CHAPTER 32

James kicked up dust as he walked with purpose towards the grave. He had slung a shovel and pick over his right shoulder, ignoring Sarah's shouts from the porch.

The previous night of terror had morphed into a bleary-eyed morning of exhaustion and fighting. James had insisted the grave should be exhumed so they could determine the state of the body within. Sarah had argued against the desecration. She presumed the act to be unholy and she feared for Carson's mental stability. James countered that Carson must stay in the house while he and George got to the bottom of the mystery.

Sarah demanded George stop James before he disinterred more than a dead body - perhaps evil spirits may have infected the dead old man.

George had ignored Sarah's request, following James out the door.

The morning sun squeezed perspiration from his arms and neck. But James remained hell bent on digging up the answers to their Chupacabra problem.

Arriving at the site, James dropped the shovel and began to pound the ax through the arid, dense soil. Plumes of dirt clouded the work area. James worked harder, using his legs and back to bring the pick down with extra force. He paused after clearing several inches of compacted earth within a three foot by five-foot rectangle. Before he could catch his breath and resume digging, George spat his tobacco and shoved James aside. The large man stuck the shovel into the ground, pounded a heavy leg upon the step and forced the blade to unearth a massive quantity of soil.

James' eyebrows danced with wonder and surprise.

George maneuvered the shovel around the framed area, lifting copious amounts of dirt out of the grave. His work continued until the shovel hit something with a cracking sound.

James and George stared at each other. George stepped away from the grave, wrestling his chaw between his cheek and gums. James knelt into the site, using his hands to feel around for what George had struck. As much as he wanted to find out what had happened to the old man, James hoped George had only struck a tree root or a large rock. His fingers stroked a smooth surface, tracing the length of the object.

"Bone." James announced his revelation without lifting his head. He scooped handfuls of dirt away until he made out the bone of an upper arm. His fingers clawed and tugged, fitting in a chasm beneath the arm. James pulled gently a few times, freeing the extremity from its resting place.

Along with the arm came the remains of the torso. James cleared more soil from the lower half of the grave, until the entire corpse was exposed. He sat back on his haunches, catching his breath, and inspecting the buried secret.

George hocked up more than tobacco juice, letting it fly with a sickening slap along the dry ground.

"Where's the head?"

James felt surprised. He had been so intent on uncovering the skeleton, he hadn't even recognized the missing part. An important part.

"It's gotta be here." James went to digging some more, searching for the piece that might reveal more clues as to the fate of the previous owner.

George commented on the condition of the body as James worked deeper. "Still has most of his skin. He ain't been dead too long."

James gave up looking for the head. He had dug deeper down and all that he found where the skull should have been was more dirt.

DESERT FANGS

"How could there be no head?"

"That dog monster took it clean off." George squinted across the fields.

"I don't understand. The lady said her husband disappeared. I assumed he had run off with another woman, or maybe he had been lost in the desert. Never figured he was killed."

George grunted. "Everyone lies. You best learn that fact sooner rather than later."

James felt his blood boil. He felt betrayed by the sweet old lady. She had duped him into buying the place. A cursed land. His anger faded into shame at having lost their entire savings on a piece of haunted dirt, with a killer beast preying on the living. And the living was the family James swore to care for. And protect.

"I'm a fool." James blinked tears away from his eyes. He knew he had to keep from crying in front of George, but his emotions had become turbulent with the new revelations.

"You ain't more fool than anyone else, kid." George scratched his beard, lowering his hat brim to shade his eyes. "Hell, you done more for your momma and Carson than most men done for others. I wouldn't fret over it."

James rose from the grave. He controlled himself from hugging George for supporting him. George was the last person James would expect to get a consoling hand from. James knew he should have counted more on George. After all, the man had traveled far and wide to hunt down his mother. Didn't that count for something? James reasoned with his thoughts.

George bent to the corpse. He rifled through the pants pockets like he expected to find some treasure. James wanted to scold George, but he realized the man wouldn't miss what he had since he was no longer among the living. George didn't find anything.

"Reckon we should put him back so he can rest and all."

James huffed. "You're right. Thanks."

George chuckled. "When I said 'we,' I meant you. Have fun." He scooped up the pickax and sauntered back toward the ranch.

James shook his head.

Now THAT'S the George I know and love.

He used the shovel to push loose soil atop the exposed body. James returned to his plan for tonight. He would bait himself for the Chupacabra. James would string himself up so it appeared he had been left to die. And when the beast came for dinner, James would plunge his blade deep into the monster's throat, opening a bloody wound so Hell could pour out.

And George would be his second. An insurance policy. Deadly with a rifle or a pistol. Somewhere within range, ready to dispatch the devil dog after James gutted it.

Or he could kill the beast after it killed James, keeping Carson and his mother safe.

There was only one wrinkle in James' plan.

He hadn't yet told George about it.

James felt the butterflies in his gut. He worried if he asked George for help, the big man would reveal the plan to his mother. And then everything would unravel.

Sarah couldn't find out what James was going to do.

He had to do what was right. James had to be a man. And men didn't clear their ideas with their mothers.

CHAPTER 33

James used his shift as lookout to implement his plan.

Alone.

After returning to the ranch with less answers than he had hoped for, James had decided to keep his plan quiet. His mother had vehemently opposed his idea. And he couldn't risk George or Lito. The more he had considered using George as a nearby backup to shoot the monster, James had become increasingly more concerned that something horrible would befall his friend. Endangering his friend and potentially breaking his mother's heart were not high priorities on his list.

The only risk worth taking was putting his own neck on the line. Literally. James had recalled how he had defeated Crouching Bear. What he had overcome to outlast Preacher. Walking down memory lane, while painful at times, built up his confidence. James had been up against impossible odds several times and had endured, victorious when death was imminent. It stood to reason that his luck would eventually run out. Nobody remained victorious forever. However, James believed in himself and his abilities.

El Chupacabra would be no different.

James waited about thirty minutes, providing enough time for everyone to drift off to sleep. Satisfied he could escape undetected, he hurried into the darkness.

The night had been eerily silent. Unlike recent evenings, screams and growls, red orbs of blinking predator eyes and the stench of death had been absent. Yet, the air had a morose quality about it. It hung with thickness, palatable and sour on the back of the tongue like a rancid piece of meat. The sensation made him nervous. But James reminded himself that nervousness honed one's senses. It was the autonomic response to something important.

He jogged on the tips of his toes in order to dampen the sounds of his footfalls. Once he arrived at the ancient cottonwood tree, James unfurled his tether. He had secreted away bailing twine so he could string himself to the trunk. Before slipping the loosened, false ties around his wrists, James unsheathed his knife. Taking a deep breath, he slowly dragged the sharpened blade along his palm. A fresh faucet of blood dampened the soil beneath his feet.

"Come and get me, you sonofabitch." He whispered into the black.

Immediately, a low rumble reverberated through his chest. James slumped against the tree. Horrific fear surged through his veins, imploring him to give up on his quest and high tail it back to the relative safety of the ranch.

It was too late.

Soft red orbs flickered to life. Dim and barely visible, the shine glowed brighter. The eyes skimmed low upon the earth and drifted higher into the night. As the glow rose to nearly the same height as James, his bladder threatened to empty.

James swallowed hard. His heart hammered in his chest. James choked back potential vomit that desired to plume from his warm, full belly.

Another grumble, strong enough to shake the tree and the ground beneath him.

James felt lightheaded. His breathing had been so erratic that he had hyperventilated to the point of blacking out.

The beast approached. Not a sound of dirt scraping under its paws. Just a ghostly growing of the creature's orbs. James marveled how the eyes hadn't blinked. Not once. It was as if the devil dog refused to lose track of its prey. The focus was nauseating.

James attempted to taunt it. Only air croaked from his lips. The words had hidden under his tongue as if they were terrified of being hunted by the same evil.

A laugh.

He gulped.

How could an animal laugh? Was it a creature from beyond the veil? Something supernatural that was beyond being killed?

James reminded himself he had faced supernatural horrors in the past. But this one was different.

He squeezed his eyes shut. James saw Carson giggling. His mother smiled; her crystal blue eyes glistened in the sun. Her long, silky black hair waved in the wind. They laughed together at the supper table. James tucked a wool blanket around Carson as they cozied under their favorite hiding tree back in Iowa. Carson reminded James to pay attention as he shuffled his deck of cards.

I should have paid better attention, Carson. I should have followed your advice. I'm so sorry, buddy.

James opened his eyes.

Its muzzle just inches from his face.

He winced at the stink of decaying meat. A smell of rotten eggs pelted James in the face. His eyes watered and his nostrils crimped to protect against the foulness.

A sticky, grimy tongue traced James' jaw like the slow caress of a familiar lover. Saliva, dripping with delicious anticipation, soaked his shirt. The wet nose gently sucked at his skin. He understood this beast enjoyed its killing. It absorbed every moment of the process, building up to its first bite.

James tried to scream but his voice failed him once again. He trembled violently. Urine flooded his dungarees in a warm gush of release. The monster growled with a chuckling tone as it must have gotten a whiff of his accident. Clearly, the beast knew it had James where it wanted him.

Dead.

Dead to rights and so terrified he had regressed to a toddler who could no longer control his bodily functions.

The wet nose buried itself into the crook of his neck. It pressed hard against his pounding jugular. James felt the razor-sharp edge of a fang as it stroked his skin. He waited for the plunging, the moment when the fang separated flesh and sinew, digging deep within the hot body, drinking deeply of the flow of life as its circular system had been diverted.

The monster dropped its head to his palm. The sticky tongue lapped up the dripping blood he had revealed to bait this creature of evil. Several slurps along his skin and then the beast was gone.

Silence.

James gasped for air. His chest heaved. He remembered his hands weren't really bound. Slipping his hands free, James fell to the earth. He buried his face in the sand, shaking and sobbing. Tears erupted like angry volcanoes.

Why didn't it kill me? How could I have been so stupid? I can't believe I am still alive.

James remained prone, shaken, for what seemed an eternity. The fear had abated. He knew if it had meant to kill him, he would have been a dried husk of meat by now.

But he wasn't.

He was still alive. It had toyed with him. Or perhaps it was a test.

But why?

James understood he was up against a force far more powerful than he had imagined. An ordinary animal would feed on what manna it was given by nature. No questions asked. There was no such thing as delayed gratification. No notion of saving for a rainy day.

Animals did what animals did. Simple.

This one had not. It had *chosen* to do something different.

Its mind had been more than animal.

James was more frightened.

And he had far more respect for El Chupacabra.

CHAPTER 34

The ranch stood stark against the grainy horizon, like a silent beacon along a treacherous shoreline. Its welcoming arms of relative safety helped to hurry James' pace. As he reached the porch, James stepped softly onto the boards, hoping to avoid attracting attention from the occupants. He strained his neck to peer where he had just narrowly escaped death.

No sign of red eyes.

Not a sound of nature stirred.

James realized he hadn't felt a sensation of being watched the whole way back. After the Chupacabra had disappeared into the shadows, James had believed he was temporarily safe. But he had been foolish. What if the creature had duped him into thinking it had gone away, only to return like a mountain lion on its fleeing deer prey?

He shivered at his lack of caution.

My whole life has been a lack of caution. I guess I prefer to run straight into trouble.

James clucked his tongue, slipped off his boots and entered the house.

The dark silence enveloped him like a warm blanket. In order to maintain his ruse, James needed to tap George for the next watch. He bit back his jealousy of the big man. After encountering the beast, James reasoned George would be up against an uneventful task. George would probably get to snooze.

He hoped he would be able to catch a few winks as well, knowing El Chupacabra might be done for the night.

Coming down the hallway, a shadow startled James. It loomed large and moved away from his mother's room.

George.

James felt his blood churn in his veins.

"What..."

George stepped aside. James couldn't believe his eyes. He strained to make out the expression on George's face but the hallway was too cloaked in darkness.

"What the hell are you up to?" James neared George with his fists clenched.

"Nothing."

James bristled at the lack of response. It sure hadn't looked like nothing to him. His friend had exited his mother's bedroom. And where James had come from, there was only one reason a man would go into his mother's private space.

"Nothing? Nothing? You expect me to believe you?" James shoved George with all his might. He had envisioned George slamming backwards into the wall.

George's body hardly nudged.

A large hand shot forward in the dark. It palmed James' face and tossed him back in the direction of the kitchen. James flailed but caught himself before dropping to the floor.

George moved forward.

"I suggest you keep your hands to yourself, kid."

James raised his fists in the air. He prepared for a fight.

"Like you? Maybe you should follow your own advice."

George grunted. "You started it."

"I mean with my mother, you overgrown sow." James almost snickered at his wicked tongue. The insult flew from a place James had not been aware of before.

"What did you call me?" George lurched forward. He grabbed James by the front of his shirt, nearly tearing the fabric from his bones.

"Get your damn hands off me." James struggled to free himself. He clawed at the large man's sizable hands with little success. "I came to send you to your shift on watch. And I find you sneaking out of her room. I'm not a fool."

"You're more a fool than you are a child." George threw James across the kitchen. His back slammed into the table, sending a sharp stabbing pain up his spine. He grabbed at his lower back. His breath came in quick gasps.

James had forgotten all about El Chupacabra. His focus had been drawn to his battle with George. A battle he had no intention of running from. James lunged at George. His hands slid down George's muscular chest, unable to find purchase. James fell at the feet of his tormentor. And he expected to lose the fight in a hurry.

To his surprise, George lifted James to his feet. He clutched James by the back of his neck and hurried him across the kitchen. James envisioned himself to be a simple broom, being walked to its place of storage. George's strength was that powerful.

"It ain't what you think. I was looking for YOU."

James stared wide at the door that was fast approaching his face.

"You was missing from YOUR watch. I checked Carson's room. Then I checked Sarah's room."

His head stopped just short of the heavy oak door. James choked on his tongue, nearly swallowing it in surprise at his good fortune.

James was spun around as easily as a toddler. He stared up into the face of his friend.

"Seems to me, you're the one with some explaining to do."

George released James. He dropped to his feet, unaware that he had been held aloft. James gulped audibly.

"I...I...well," James stammered. His mind emptied, unable to conjure a lie to keep himself from getting a whooping.

How did this turn against me?

James rubbed saliva from his lips with the back of his sleeve.

"What is all this noise?"

Sarah stood on the far side of the kitchen with her arms folded across her nightdress. James could sense her aggravation by the tone in her voice. George turned to face his mother. James peered around the large man's shoulder to face his new problem.

"Nothing. Sorry we woke you."

Sarah tapped her foot. "You probably woke everyone in town. You've been so dang loud. Now what is going on here?"

"Your boy accused me of crimes I ain't done committed. Ain't that right, James? Why don'tcha tell your mother what you said to me." George stepped aside, as if providing enough space for James to face his judge and jury.

Probably my executioner as well.

James wanted to blurt out his suspicions but he feared hurting his mother's feelings. Even if she were guilty of whoring with George, it wouldn't be appropriate for him to accuse his mother of behaving indecently. And what if he was wrong? The consequences would be far more severe. Something in the way George had just spoken cast doubt in James' mind. Perhaps he HAD jumped to conclusions. What if George HAD been looking for James? All paths of escaping the predicament had been eclipsed by his lack of clarity. James didn't know what was truthful.

James chuckled nervously. "Aw, you know how guys are. I was messing around and I forgot how bad George's temper got."

Sarah tilted her head at George as if she knew she was being fed a line and she expected George to give her the real story.

"Pardon us for a moment."

George grabbed James by the back of his neck again. He opened the door and carried James through to the porch. James had a hunch the discussion had not ended.

The slamming door behind them signaled as much.

CHAPTER 35

James found himself flying through the air. As he floated on his back, James watched the stars above twinkle along a brightening canopy. He landed hard. The air expelled from his lungs in a gushing wheeze. For a brief moment, the lights went out in his mind.

George was upon him before he could catch his breath. His body rose high in the air, lingered for a second, and then plummeted directly down to the dirt he had just been lying in. James felt his teeth clank together almost shattering them in half from the brunt force of his body colliding with the ground.

Through the haze in his mind, James heard his mother shout for them to stop fighting.

James rolled to his knees, struggling to rise to his attacker. Sand and soil clung to the saliva along his lips. Choking to get air into his lungs, James swallowed clouds of dust. He heard the approaching boots, forcing himself to move faster than his body could recover.

George's foot swung wide, narrowly missing where James' stomach had been moments ago.

Carson squeaked past Sarah onto the porch. James witnessed the concern in his little buddy's face. He knew he had to make a good showing in this fight or he'd lose all the respect Carson had for him.

James threw a wild punch. It hardly grazed the side of George's face. He set himself for another strike. His hands up, James deflected a jab. He cocked his fist and landed a solid punch to a jaw that felt like a brick.

George groaned. James smirked. He knew the strike had caused his friend pain. But his self-appreciation ended just as quickly. George clobbered James in the cheek with a hook.

His knees buckled and gave way. James crumpled to the ground. The stars floating before his eyes were indiscernible from the ones in the night sky. George stood over James. He bent over, glaring at James.

"I said stop it. Right now." Sarah shouted from the porch. Lito had joined her and Carson as spectators. The stocky guest hobbled down the steps on his way to the combatants.

James raised his hand to his face. He rubbed along the spot where George had hit him. A wavy streak of blood coated his flesh.

"You bleeding, mi amigo." Lito pointed towards James.

Remembering his self-inflicted wound, James tried to wipe the blood from his face. Instead, his actions spread the stain further.

George shuffled closer. James understood his only chance for winning the fight with George would require ingenuity. Toe to toe, George would pummel James into oblivion. If James could employ guerilla tactics, then he stood a chance.

James swept his right leg across his body. The heel of his boot caught George's shin, toppling the large man. As he struck the earth, George emitted a groan of pain. James shimmied to his knees and crawled like a spider across a hot tin plate. He attempted to climb atop George but was met with extreme resistance. George's huge, calloused hands clutched at James' throat. He squeezed and lifted, forcing James to gasp for air. James' hands flew to his neck, laboring to peel George's fingers from his throat. In the background, James heard Lito mumble something in Spanish. Sarah continued to shout for them to stop fighting. But James ignored the external stimuli. All his energy targeted the hands that strangled him.

Using his knee, James jabbed his leg into George's ribs. The first blow hadn't slowed George's anger. The next knee caused an anguished grunt. Each successive knee loosened George's grasp. The last one released the pressure as George rolled away to protect his sensitive wound. James dropped to the dust. He remained on all fours, gasping for oxygen. As far as he was concerned, the fight was over. He couldn't take much more of the beating, especially if it came down to choosing to breathe.

A temporary stalemate wedged between the combatants. George rose to his feet, hunched over and clasping his ribs. His face contorted in pain. James stayed on his knees, shoulders rising and falling rapidly to facilitate the intake of more air. His forehead wrinkled in shock at nearly being strangled.

"Enough." James huffed.

"I don't take orders from you, kid." George stepped closer.

"He's right." Sarah stepped off the porch. "It's enough already. We're a family, dammit."

James tossed his head in the direction of his mother. He wondered what she meant by family. She and Carson were his family. Not George. George was just a friend. If she considered George part of the family, then maybe there was more to it than met the eye.

All the more reason for my accusation.

James rose. He glared at his mother. "I'm just protecting our family, mother."

"From George?" Sarah crossed her arms.

"From everything. That's why I went out there tonight. I wanted to face the beast before it can hurt any of you."

"Where did you go?" Sarah's tone shifted to disapproval.

James realized he had said too much. He hadn't wished to reveal what he had been up to. It would be no surprise how his mother and Carson would react to his foolishness.

A large hand landed on his shoulder and spun James around. George stood inches from James' face. "Better start talking."

James gulped. "Wait. Just wait." He backed up to put some distance between him and George. "I only laid a trap for the Chupacabra."

"Plenty of traps around, James." George's eyes burrowed under James' flesh. "You're lying."

"I did it for all of you." James cast his eyes downward, fearing reproach.

"Did what," Sarah asked.

James bit his lower lip. He knew he was caught. It would be a matter of minimizing the damage, covering just enough tracks…

George clutched James by the shirt collars. He pulled James within an inch of his face. James nearly gagged from the smell of musty tobacco and morning breath.

"You got one second to come clean, kid."

James gulped. He wished he were tethered out in the dark, taking his chances with the beast rather than facing more punishment at George's hands.

"I used myself as bait. To trap the Chupacabra. Get it close enough so I could..."

"So you could what? Become a corpse?" George gritted his teeth.

"James. How dare you risk your life. Everything." Sarah's eyes filled with terror.

"No, amigo. No hay trabajo."

James ignored Lito's Spanish. He waited for the recrimination to come forward from Carson's lips.

George tossed James into the dirt, standing ominously above. James twisted on his rump, searching for Carson's presence. The knots in his stomach signaled an eerie sensation of foreboding.

"Where's Carson?"

The four adults realized the boy had disappeared. All anger dissipated as the search began for the missing child.

CHAPTER 36

It was all his fault. He had been the one to find George in town. He had found the grave out in the fields. And his protection had caused too much stress for James and Sarah. Carson wanted to be a contributing member of the family. He yearned for the days when he and James had shared chores in the saloon. Times when life had been simpler and more fun. Playing, hiding, dreaming.

Their lust for adventure.

Instead, they had moved multiple times to places far away and unimaginable. Starting over each time. Becoming more serious and grown up.

The good old days.

Now, Carson must live up to expectations. He had to save James from the immense responsibilities and pressures of looking after a household. Carson couldn't verbalize his understanding of their situation but he had figured out the gravity of their predicament by paying attention to the verbal cues. And the words.

James had gone to fight the Screeper all alone. He had risked his life and now everyone was mad at James. Even Carson.

It hurt his feelings to know James would so easily leave him behind. After all they had talked about over the years. Teaming up to take on evil and save mankind from the bad actors in the world. Carson had always looked up to James, most times worshiping his older friend. But he had considered them both equals when it came to fighting the injustices of the West. And for James to leave him flat, Carson had been crushed. His heart wept for being overlooked.

They were supposed to be a team.

Carson ran in a wide arc through the thick darkness. He circled around the back of the ranch to avoid being detected by the family. The fear in his belly of being all alone in the night was overruled by his desire to prove himself to James. Carson figured if the Screeper snagged him now, at least he could hold his head high as a contributing member of the family. He imagined James and Sarah standing over his small grave, dabbing tears from their cheeks as they asked God for answers to his death. He would miss them so much but he would stand tall in heaven knowing he had done the right thing.

A prickly scrub brush scratched Carson's flesh as he collided with the unseen obstacle. He rolled along the dirt, quickly jumping back to his feet to continue his journey. With a shaky hand, Carson rubbed the surface wound and gritted his teeth against an anguished cry.

He had to reach his destination.

Carson knew the Screeper was close by. And there were very few places the monster would haunt as it hunted for its next meal. He counted on three potential traps. His gut told him near which one the Screeper would most likely meet up with him.

He leaned into the night to increase his speed, enjoying the slight breeze that ruffled his hair and cooled his sweaty skin.

Carson squinted to avoid any other roadblocks. Running face first into a tree trunk or tripping over a large rock could derail his plans before he got started. His memory of the land from countless hours of playing in the yard and carrying out his chores provided a mental compass against stumbling blocks.

The night sky lightened a tad, shedding a soft glow on the vast landscape. Not enough to clarify the surroundings but enough to expose shapes against the horizon. The increased visibility strengthened Carson's resolve. He felt more confident of reaching his destination.

The grave site.

Carson neared the spot. He found it difficult to locate the leaning, make-shift cross in the darkness. Slowing down his pace, he kicked a clump of fabric. Carson knelt down, patting the earth at his feet. His fingers traced the ragged outline of the crumpled hat that had once hung from the wood marker.

He had arrived.

For the first time since he had run away, Carson listened to the air around him. Between his gasps for breath, the night was eerily silent. No chirping crickets. No coyote howls. Not even a whisper of night breeze.

His skin dimpled with the chill that traced his spine. He felt an urge to pee himself. Squeezing his knees together, Carson quelled his bladder's need for relief.

Carson tried to call out to the Screeper. He wanted to announce his position to lure the monster out of hiding. Only a crackling squeak passed his lips. His tongue was dry and he choked as he attempted to swallow without saliva.

An odd vibration rumbled inside his chest. The feeling brought Carson to his knees. He gasped and fought a wave of nausea. His eyes darted along the horizon for any signs of movement. Carson knew he was no longer alone. He felt it deep in his bones. But the Screeper revealed little about its hiding spot.

"Here..." Carson's mind completed the sentence where his words had failed him.

"Here I am."

He crawled forward, fingers tickling the earth to find the wooden cross. He traced the marker down to where earth met limb. Carson clutched at the base like he was hanging on for dear life, dangling over the edge of a precipice. Even with solid terra firma beneath him, Carson felt as if he were treading water in a deep, boundless ocean with no support to help him.

Something moved to his right.

Carson breathed rapidly. He squeezed his eyes against the coming danger. All notions of bravery and proving his self-worth to James evaporated immediately. Out here, Carson felt all alone. Unsafe. Petrified.

He wished he had stayed in the house, never hearing the commotion on the porch that had awakened him from his slumber. He should have stayed in bed, tugging the pillow down tight over his ears to block out the noise of the commotion.

Asleep in his bed, under a blanket and nestled into the wall, Carson would have lived through the night.

Now, he hoped to live through the next few minutes.

Another shuffling sound. This time behind him.

Carson sobbed into the crook of his arm. His grip on the wooden cross tightened, forcing his fingers to turn bone white. As tears filled his eyes, Carson tried to recall the prayers of the preachers from church. A few words came to him, disjointed and out of order.

"Please, please, please."

He whispered into the dark, hoping God would hear him before it was too late.

CHAPTER 37

James stumbled into Lito. He shoved the smaller man aside to move onward in his search for Carson. Without waiting for his mother or George, James jumped over the porch railing.

The first place they had looked, Carson's room, had been empty. They had split up and covered each room of the house, looking under beds and behind doors. Sarah had cried out in an ear-piercing noise. The sound had unnerved James.

The three of them met up in the kitchen, confirming their failure to locate the missing boy. James noticed Lito peeking through the open door from the porch. He had remained in place while the others had scoured the home. James shoved aside some anger toward Lito for not aiding the search party.

"Where could he have gone?" Sarah wringed her hands together.

"He can't have gone far." George stuffed a fresh wad of tobacco leaves into the corner of his mouth.

James tried to focus his mind. The panic has been disconcerting and his mother's reaction coupled with George's ruggedness kept James on edge. He wondered how Carson could have slipped away when he had been tucked neatly between Sarah and Lito on the porch.

A vision of El Chupacabra snatching Carson from the porch boards danced in his mind's eye.

"If he didn't come back in here, then he must've gone into the yard."

Sarah rushed to the door. She peered over Lito's head.

"Maybe he went to the pen."

"Yo no se."

James hurled himself through the doorway, narrowly beating George to the punch.

Sprinting for the animal's pen, James quickly distanced himself from George, who struggled to keep up with him. The much bigger man had fighting skills and strength but he lacked speed. James reached the pen to find Tina and the rest of the hogs happily snoozing in a corner. A few of the goats were milling about, staring back at James with aloof expressions as they chewed their cud.

Sarah and Lito pulled up the rear. George huffed and coughed. James shifted his attention to the fields surrounding the pen.

"I think we should split up to cover more ground. We need to check the other side of the house. And the rock pile that way." James pointed across the back yard. He refused to let Carson disappear on his watch.

What could've gotten into him? Why would he run off?

James decided to bark out orders rather than wait for everyone to step up.

"Mother, you check the back of the house and make sure you look in the cottonwoods out front. Carson might have climbed into one of them."

Sarah nodded and turned back on her way.

"Lito, you head to the tree line along the far edge of the property. Don't be afraid to poke your head into the woods, too. Carson probably wouldn't go far inside, but he'd dig himself under the brush if it seemed a good hiding spot."

Lito ran off with a waddling gait.

"You got orders for me, too, kid?"

James glared at George. He knew their confrontation was far from over. He wanted to sock George in the jaw but he couldn't waste more time than they had already.

"Yeah, you come with me. We're going to the rock outcropping. I think it is our best chance at finding him."

"You really think he would go that far?" George spat a gusher of chew juice.

James quickly considered George's point. "No, but if there is a place I fear the most, it's that lump of rocks. And I know Carson enjoys climbing over it."

Without waiting for a response, James hightailed it for the boulders. He heard George curse and grumble under his breath. A smirk of satisfaction spread across James' lips. If he couldn't strike George now, then he would at least enjoy the satisfaction of frustrating the bigger man.

James felt his dander stand on end. Something didn't feel right. The thickness of danger enveloped him. His heart stung from the fear of losing Carson.

What if the Chupacabra got him?

James ignored the question until more questions ran through his mind.

How would he ever forgive himself? Would his mother be able to look him in the eye if something dreadful had befallen their little friend?

He ignored the potential answers to each thought. As the sky lightened ever so slightly, James stared at the looming outcropping along the horizon. His feet moved with lightning quickness and still James felt as if he tread through a mucky swamp.

Nearing the rocks, James steered himself toward the center, where the crevices provided the most convenient footholds. He shouted over his shoulder for George to trace the lower edge of the rocks. James couldn't wait for George to catch up. He straddled the bumpy cracks and nooks, pulling himself upward to the top. James carefully jogged along the top of the massive rocks, trying to cover as much area as he could without breaking his neck.

A hole opened before him. James noticed the gap just in time to hurl his body across the chasm. He landed with a bone-crunching thud on the far side of the rock. James winced at the sharp pain in his elbows and knees. He rubbed his scraped hands along his dungarees.

That was a close one.

James climbed to his feet. He paused, turning in circles to scout the top of the pile without endangering himself further.

He heard George call up to him. George hadn't found Carson along the lower rim of the rocks. James deflated as the emptiness of his own search matched George's.

"Dang it." James caught his breath for a moment. "I'm coming down."

James found the trek down more treacherous than going up. Climbing, the body leaned toward the rocks and provided him with more stability. Going down, his weight leaned away from the pile and the footholds became much less obvious.

As he reached the bottom, James rested against the wall. His mind raced to think of other places Carson could have gone. He hoped he had been wrong and his mother had found Carson nestled into a tree close to the house.

"Each minute that passes lowers our chances."

James grimaced at George's positivity. "We have to keep looking."

"Years of tracking game... The longer they ain't found, the more likely they ain't gonna be found."

The truth of the matter stung James. He knew George was right. But he couldn't give up on Carson. Not yet.

He owed everything to the boy. And if anything happened to him, it would be on James' conscious.

Forever.

CHAPTER 38

The alpha lurked in the darkest shadows. It caught the scent on the wind. A subtle, sweet smell. Faint and delicious, filled with promise of pleasure and nourishment. It licked the saliva dripping from its anticipating lips.

After toying with the kill, the alpha had slinked off to a copse of briars to contemplate the next move. And to ruminate on the potential miscalculation of letting the prey go. A hunter's skill rested with the intuition of when the kill was appropriate. Deer hunters would just as soon pass on a shot if the slightest bit of doubt remained that the mark would not land true. They would lower the rifle's hammer and wait for a better moment, when the kill shot was a guarantee to bring home protein without leaving a wounded animal behind.

Yet, the alpha had the certain kill shot.

The man had been there for the taking. Definite protein. With no chance of outrunning the predator, the human was primed for death.

Something hadn't felt right.

And the excitement of the hunt was missing. The choice to let the man walk had been easy because there had been no fun in finding him. No hunt. Missing screams and beating hearts. Without chase and struggle. The hunter couldn't accept an easy kill.

It would have been unnatural.

Picking up the new trail, the alpha lifted its snout to the sky, drinking in the metallic odor that beckoned it. A new body. Warm. Scared. Pounding surges in its veins.

The boy.

The alpha recognized the smell. The sweet milk of youth that had tempted it days ago. So young and fresh. Tender meat. Blood so pure it was like crystalline spring water.

Movement along the expanse fixed the alpha's attention. It watched as the small creature ran to and fro, stumbling awkwardly over brambles and stones.

The hunt was on.

The thirst unquenchable.

It grinned through fangs of ancient bone as it realized the wait would soon end. And the decision to allow the man to live would be rewarded. The best part, the alpha knew, would be the next battle when the man would come with a heart full of rage and revenge. THAT hunt would be well worth the delayed gratification.

The boy stopped traveling when he reached the old man's monument. He crouched down and fumbled with the dried sticks. The beating heart betraying dread and something else...

Guilt?

The alpha shrugged off the game of figuring out what the dying soul felt. It no longer cared about anything in its surroundings. Only the boy. Only the kill. Only the blood.

Silently, the alpha tiptoed closer. Each step heightening the overpowering stench of fear and crimson. The anticipation became dizzying.

The boy whimpered. He spoke through gasps and croaks. Soft and scared. The alpha strained to listen for coming danger. No other presence was detected. The beast pinned its ears back and moved in for the meal. The saliva thickened and drooled from its maw, unable to turn off the faucet of the dinner bell. It neared the boy.

The heart pounded, heavy and increasingly loud. So strong in the frail frame, yet able to reverberate along the alpha's scent glands.

Another soft whimper.

The alpha stepped in. It slowly inhaled an enormous breath. The boy's pores dripped with horror, further inciting the beast. It extended its dripping tongue to taste the flesh of the child.

Delectable.

The meat trembled uncontrollably under the soft, slick texture of the alpha's tongue. The excitement blossomed into an orgiastic desire. The time had arrived. No further delays. It had to eat now.

The alpha sliced a quick gash along the arm of the child. Slight but true. The taste of the blood overwhelmed the alpha. It had never tasted anything so sweet before. Never. Another fang dragged along the opened wound, leaving a crisscross of torn flesh. The blood flowed more freely. Still a trickle compared to a deep feeding. But satisfying, nonetheless.

The alpha wished to enjoy the meal. It determined to use superficial wounds as the appetizer before opening the skin to feed on the gore.

The boy began to fight back. He released his death grip on the crucifix to push away the beast's snout. The alpha enjoyed the play. It chuckled through its fangs, forcing its muzzle to burrow tighter. The cords in its neck bulked to keep the pressure down, warding off the weak attempts of the child.

The struggle brought more blood to the surface. Again, the alpha grunted with pleasure. The boy was too defective to understand that more life force only drained more blood. The boy would have been wise to play dead, saving his blood and life.

Silly child.

As it drank from the surface of the skin, the alpha chose the next shot placement.

It released the boy. The child crawled away from the grave site, crying to a deity that would not come to his pleas for salvation. The exposed lower leg tempted the alpha. As the dungarees rolled up, the alpha lunged forward. With soft meat revealed, the alpha bit into the pulsing calf muscle. Juices flooded its maw. Backing off from severing the meat to the bone, the alpha lapped up freshly spilled nectar. The boy used his free leg to kick against the alpha's skull. The first kick landed hard, angering the beast. It swallowed down the rage with a large gulp of crimson and shifted its body so that its rear stood between the feeding and the raised leg of the child. Continuous kicks hardly disturbed the beast as it drank more life from the frail body.

The child relented, giving into the inevitable demise of existence on this earth. The alpha sensed it through the skin's conductivity, as well as the lack of struggle. The blood's flavor soured slightly. It would need to finish the feeding soon to fully enjoy the meal before death settled in.

The alpha dropped the leg from its jaws. It turned to face the crying face of the child. Stepping over the body, the alpha dripped a mixture of saliva and blood into the eyes of the boy. It stared down at the throbbing jugular, the most precious cut of meat.

The alpha could no longer contain its desires.

It bent to finish what it had started.

The fangs closed in around the boy's throat. It rolled its eyes back in its skull as the tips of razor-sharp weapons dug down.

CHAPTER 39

Sarah charged at James. She swung an open palm at his face but missed when he ducked to the right. James backed away with a surprised expression. The look on his face further aggravated her. Sarah charged at him again.

George stepped in front of Sarah. His massive chest forced her head to snap back.

"What is wrong with you?"

"What is wrong with ME?" Sarah tried to get at James. George clasped enormous hands over her wrists and held her in place. She strained her neck to glare around the wall of man at her son. "YOU are the reason we are in this mess. YOU are the reason for *every* mess we land in."

James removed his hat and dabbed sweat from his brow. "I'm trying to find Carson, mother."

Sarah yanked her arms free from George. "Carson is missing because of YOU."

The words had escaped before she could temper her anger. As a parent, she felt awful for pinning all their problems on her son. But she couldn't help her feelings of frustration. She was scared for Carson's life.

And she had been overwhelmed with worry for their family since striking out for Texas. The move had been James' idea. He had insisted they start fresh. James had implored them to go along with his plan for a simpler life. An existence free of battles against evil. A happy life of farming and husbandry. A life of working for themselves and not slaving for meager wages at the hand of powerful master.

She had gone along with him.

Sarah had fallen in love with James' optimism and his dreamy fantasies. What else could she have done, after all she had been through. Life had been hard up to that point and she, too, had grown weary of the death and the constant danger.

"Can you give us a minute?" Sarah begged George and Lito for a chance to speak with her son without the benefit of an audience.

George passed looks between James and Sarah, quietly nodded and stepped away. Lito followed just as silently.

"We don't have time to discuss this." James attempted to brush past Sarah.

She clutched his arm.

"James, I can't do this. I love you and I want to make a home for our family. But I can't keep fighting for...for our lives."

James grabbed her arms, negating Sarah's hold on his.

"We need to find Carson. Can we talk later?"

"There might not be a later, James." She choked back some tears. Sarah broke free of James' grasp and turned her back to him. "Everywhere we go. Everything we do. It all leads to horror."

Sarah spun to look James in the face.

"Life has always been hard for us. But chasing these dreams of being like your father is going to get us killed. Your daddy is a lucky man. A man who makes his own luck. He's different than us. Don't you see?"

James fidgeted, obviously preoccupied with locating Carson.

Sarah understood the urgency of continuing the search. But she had to make her stand now, while the emotions were raw. Otherwise, she would knuckle under and follow along in the hopes of pleasing her son and maintaining appearances for an ideal family life.

They had never been an ideal family.

"I'm sorry, mother. I will change. But I need to find him. Now."

Sarah nodded through the tears. She felt the typical softening in her heart.

She'd never be able to escape James' wild ride.

James kissed her cheek and ran to catch up with George and Lito.

Sarah sobbed into her palm. Their doom was a fate she would have to embrace. James lived a reckless life. He meant well. But he was still a boy in a man's body. A lack of male role models in his formative years cursed him to forever be a child in mind.

The qualities of youth were endearing. James had an aura to his personality that people naturally gravitated towards. He had been popular in the towns they had lived in. Courteous and bold. But his choices had been impetuous. And Sarah couldn't see James changing any time soon.

She hurried after James, suddenly aware of her own danger being left behind in the darkness. That monster was still out there, somewhere.

Carson.

Sarah sniffled hard as she ran. She prayed silently that Carson was alive. Hiding in a new spot because he was afraid of their shouting. Safe from the devil that hunted life from every angle of the desert.

When she found him, Sarah resolved to hold Carson in her arms and not let go. She'd have to figure out how to force change in James. Or come up with a plan to leave him behind. It would break her heart to walk away from her son, her life. Sarah couldn't continue to fight on at the pace of his life. She had grown older and less energetic. Setting down some deep roots and living a boring, tedious life is all she wanted. Sarah had been lucky to get away from whoring, being used up by callous men. Some of them even struck her and took advantage of her softer body. Most of the girls died in the business. They either withered slowly under the pain of syphilis or they died suddenly at the hands of a ruthless owner or a violent trick.

Sarah had weathered raising a boy without a father. She'd kept him sheltered from the harsher aspects of the western expansion. And as much as she had worked to make him a better human being than most others, his fate ran straight for him. Regardless of her efforts.

James was an Earp.

Through and through. He had a lust for life and an adventurous spirit. Sarah wondered if he could last as long as his daddy. The number of barrels the man had stared down. The fights he had ended. The towns he had brought to heel.

In her heart of hearts, Sarah hoped James would outlive his daddy. She prayed he would mature beyond the wild curiosity that flowed in his veins.

Sarah shook her head and wiped the tears from her cheeks with the back of her sleeves. There would be plenty of time for contemplation and planning.

Hopefully.

Right now, she had to find Carson.

If anything bad happened to him...

Sarah refused to finish her thought.

CHAPTER 40

The scuffle placed an exclamation point on an already stressful evening. James had snuck off to deal with El Chupacabra on his own. George had lost his temper with James' insinuations and lack of teamwork. Sarah had erupted in an emotional tirade aimed at James.

And Carson had gone missing.

George walked away from the family spat slowly. He kept an ear trained over his shoulder to monitor Sarah. If James chose to lift a hand against his own mother, then George would box his ears like none other. In his gut, George knew there would be no possibility of such an occurrence. James might be misguided but he was respectful of women and his loved ones.

His thoughts turned to Carson. He couldn't fathom where the boy had run to. Or why he had disappeared. If the Chupacabra had snatched up the kid, then George would...

"Vamos."

George stopped in his tracks. He scolded Lito for using Spanish. "You gonna keep talking like a chicken or are you gonna talk normal?"

"Que?" Lito raised a hand to his mouth, realizing he had spoken in Spanish once more. "Sorry. We go now."

"Go where?"

Lito swung a chubby arm in a wide circle. "We look for nino."

George squinted across the landscape. His mind rattled through potential places the kid could've gone. He checked off a mental inventory of the spots they had already checked. The front yard. The animal pen. The wooded lot. The rocky outcropping. George surmised there couldn't have been many more places as most of the land was flat and pretty barren.

"You go check the front yard again. Sarah may have missed something in her panic."

"No necessito. You come con mi."

George spat. "There you go again with that danged jabberin'. I told you to go on."

Lito stood his ground. "No. He no there."

Clenching his fists, George bit into the wad of leaf inside his mouth. He was quickly losing patience with the little Mexican. He respected the man's will to stand up to him, but, in the end, George knew he would impose his will on the smaller man.

"How do you know where Carson is? Did you do something to him?" George grabbed Lito's shirt and tugged the man up to his level. Lito's feet dangled off the ground. "Why sure. That's it, ain't it? You come along and now this family has big problems. I knew you couldn't be trusted."

Lito shook nervously. He raised his hands up in a praying gesture. "No, por favor. Vamos."

George smirked. "I'll va-mouse you, you piece of donkey dung."

He tossed Lito to the ground. The heavy man crashed with a plop into the dirt. Lito rolled over and grabbed the hat that had fallen from his head. George moved fast with his fists balled into fleshy mallets.

"The boy. He no here. I show you. Come."

Lito scrambled to his feet and waddled away quickly. George had been surprised by the spritely speed of the little man. He pursued Lito as fast as he could. He wouldn't let the Mexican get away with what he had done to Carson. Nor would he allow a foreigner to speak to him like that.

Catching the smaller man by the shoulder, George gripped Lito and spun him around. "What did you do with Carson? Show me where he is before I string you up in a tree and whip you like a rogue bronco."

"The grave. The boy. He grave."

George's stomach sank. Had the Mexican killed Carson and buried him? He hoped the confession would lead him to Carson's body so he could get on with the killing. George didn't want to face Sarah with the bad news. But he would enjoy each cry of anguish he could summon from the punishment Lito would receive.

"You killed him?" George punched Lito in the face. The small man's head jerked back with a thunderous slapping sound. George watched the eyes glaze over and roll backwards as Lito dropped to the ground. He hurried over to Lito's body. With one hand, George snatched Lito's chest into the air, his head lolling from side to side. George cocked another fist over his shoulder to strike again.

Lito slowly raised his head. His eyes struggled to stay open. "The boy. He found grave of old man. He went to grave. Not dead."

George dropped Lito. He realized he had misunderstood Lito's meaning. All along, George figured Lito had been confessing to murder. Instead, he had offered a new place for them to search. George felt guilty for tossing the man around. He shrugged his shoulders when he remembered Lito was a man from another country.

Too bad.

George picked Lito up and supported his wobbly legs. "Ain't no time to take a nap. Show me where this danged grave is."

Lito rubbed his jaw and tested the muscles as he opened and closed his mouth several times. "I show."

George assisted Lito as the man pointed in the general direction of the grave site.

"You better be right about this. If we don't find Carson there, I might have to get nasty with you."

Lito gulped. "More nasty?"

"That was a love-tap, senorito. You ain't seen nasty yet."

Lito groaned. George half-carried, half-dragged Lito toward the far field. He felt along his side with his free arm, checking to be sure his pistol and knife were still at the ready. The thought of meeting the creature unprepared churned his belly into knots. And he didn't want to waste any more time returning to get his trusty weapons.

George remembered Sarah and James had been left behind to carry on over the family business. He hoped they had hashed out their differences and were on the way to back them up. Sarah and James wouldn't know where he and Lito had gone so George had to get their attention. But without warning the beast of their location.

He let loose an imitation of a whippoorwill. George knew the sound wasn't indigenous to the region but he hoped the sound would further differentiate it as a call to come along on his trail. James probably had no idea what a whippoorwill sounded like. Sarah probably hadn't heard one before either.

George kept the call going as he hurried Lito toward the grave. The man's feet were coming back to him and George was grateful he could save more of his strength for whatever he might find waiting for them at the site.

Would they find Carson? Would he be alive? Or dead?

He hoped for Lito's sake, Carson would be sleeping like a baby in a cradle.

CHAPTER 41

James and Sarah caught up with George and Lito. After a brief reconciliation, George told them about Lito's idea of how to find Carson. They hadn't even considered the grave site of the previous owner. All along, James figured Carson would have gone to places he enjoyed playing. Carson was very much a creature of habit. And he never wasted time with things he didn't find fun.

Across the flat land, a shadow darted off. James squinted to see if he could follow the shape but it was gone in the blink of an eye. He inventoried what the shadow could have been. It moved too fast to be Carson. And the shape had been odd. Large, like a cow perhaps. But James knew a cow couldn't move at that speed either.

Nobody else seemed to notice the shadow. The search party had their eyes focused on the ground ahead of them. James opened his mouth to reveal what he had seen. He thought better of it because he didn't want to alarm anyone. In the dark, his eyes could have been playing tricks on him. Instead, James picked up his pace and ran ahead of the rest of the group.

Before he knew it, James had come upon the grave. He made out the shape of a body lying on the ground. As he neared it, the wooden grave marker, leaning askew and frail, signaled he had arrived.

Carson.

The boy was spread-eagled along the hard soil. James hollered to the group pulling up the rear. He waved them to hurry forward. James strained to see Carson's face. He picked up Carson's head to lift him closer when he realized the warm dampness along the boy's neck.

Blood.

"No, no, no." James shouted as he turned Carson's head in his hands. The boy remained listless. Lifeless.

James gently placed Carson's head down and scrambled to pull off his neckerchief. He quickly fastened it into a narrow band and fed it beneath Carson's neck. He wrapped it around and pulled it tight, tight enough to constrict the blood flow but not too tight as to choke off Carson's breathing.

The group had arrived. Sarah threw herself into the dirt and shoved James aside. She squeezed Carson into her arms and tucked his face against her breast. Her cries broke the night and James could almost hear her tears streaming down her cheeks.

He felt around Carson's dangling arm for a pulse. It was a struggle with Sarah rocking the boy back and forth in her arms. James implored Sarah to remain still long enough for him to check. The beat in Carson's wrist was faint. Almost non-existent.

He's alive.

James pulled his fingers away, again finding blood on his hands. Carson had been bitten on the neck and wrists.

"We need to get him back to the ranch immediately. He's still alive. We don't have much time."

"You can't save him. He's lost too much blood." George scratched at his stubble, his voice shaky with emotion.

"We WILL save him. He can't die." James rose to face George.

Sarah wailed louder. Her sorrow shook the men in their boots. James knelt beside Sarah and rubbed her back. She tucked her wet face into his shoulder. James swallowed his own tears and worked to determine their plan. They had to get Carson to safety. The boy needed poultices and bandages to clean the wounds and stem the bleeding.

And then what?

James' mind leaped ahead to the Chupacabra. It had become extremely personal now. The creature had haunted them from afar, or at least, far enough that they hadn't been attacked. But now it had brought death to their door. And of all the people it could've harmed...

Carson.

James jumped to his feet. He pulled Sarah up and shook her. "We have to go. Now."

George moved closer. He snatched Carson from Sarah's arms, cradling the boy as if he were a dangerous stack of dynamite and made for the ranch. James coddled Sarah as he followed behind George. Their pace was slower but he nudged her along as best he could so they could arrive simultaneously.

She was devastated. James couldn't recall a time when his mother had felt so frail and broken down. For the first time in his life, James witnessed his mother's aging. She had always been a strong, fiery woman. Bigger than him until recent years. But even as he had grown into a man, his mother had remained the backbone of the family. The strength behind their lives. To see her in this condition, to feel her trembling and weak against his body shook him to his core.

James would see to it that vengeance would be paid in full. Not only for his little buddy Carson. But for his mother, too. He would go to hell and back in order to kill the monster that had torn apart their family.

It's not the Chupacabra's fault. It's yours.

James winced at his subconscious. The truth in the internal voice rang loudly like a church bell on Sunday. It had been his fault. He had moved them to Texas. He had purchased the cursed land, knowing full well of the rumors behind the affordable land. And he had chosen to do it anyway. His overconfidence and pride as the "head of the household" had led him right into the jaws of the devil himself.

"Hurry." James barked at his mother and George. The words stated as much to spur them on as to silence the voices in his head.

George grumbled something unintelligible under his breath. Sarah lifted her head from James' shoulder and moved forward with more of her own power than before. His command must have wakened her from the terror of their situation, reminding her of their duty to save Carson's life.

James clutched his mother's hand, running alongside her as they caught up to George. The ranch was beginning to come into view. His mind shifted to the implements he would need to collect for Sarah to nurse Carson back to health. He'd need cloth for bandages first. Then he would need to get a bucket of water. And start a fire. They'd need warm water to clean the wounds. James wished he had some of the healing abilities of the shaman he had encountered so long ago.

They reached the porch. George kicked the door wide. He took Carson to his room and laid him down in his bed. Sarah grabbed a pot and a towel from the stove.

The race was on to bring Carson back to life.

CHAPTER 42

The sight of his hosts in their moment of despair affected Lito. He felt as traumatized as they appeared. It would be such a tragedy to bury the simple-minded boy in any scenario. Especially because of El Chupacabra.

Lito understood the devastation the beast could bring. He had seen it in his own country. He had heard tales as a youngster. The nightmares of his youth had been as real as if the monster had come to him in his wakefulness. The horror had always remained present wherever he traveled.

He watched them hurry back to the ranch. After a few paces, Lito stopped in his tracks. He decided not to follow them. In his mind, he had not done enough to help this family rid themselves of the curse. It was his fault that El Chupacabra still hunted them.

Lito scanned the horizon for El Chupacabra. He knew it was out there. Watching. Waiting. El Chupacabra would be back to pick them off. One by one.

No tiempo.

He ran as fast as his stocky legs would take him, which wasn't much faster than a waddling shuffle.

The cottonwood tree loomed like a scarecrow with long broken arms swaying above the compact soil. Lito found the strap James had used to tie himself to the limbs. When James had recounted the story about trying to lure El Chupacabra to the tree, Lito couldn't imagine how anybody could sacrifice themselves to the devil like that. In the same location, Lito couldn't imagine NOT doing it to save the wonderful family.

He tugged the rope to ensure it would be strong enough to hold his weight. Lito knew when EL Chupacabra came, he would try to run for his life. He had never been a brave soul and when the time to die arrived, Lito was smart enough to understand his nature. He'd flee. But, if the ropes held tight, Lito would stay in place to face El Diablo.

Tightening the rope around his left wrist, Lito began to have second thoughts. He wished to help James and Sarah, maybe not so much George. But he would be risking his life. The odds were stacked against him. El Chupacabra was a killing machine, designed to devour its way through centuries of human flesh. And he was just a mortal man. Scared and not very strong.

Lito slapped his cheek with his free hand. He had to focus on his plan. Lito pulled the knot tight and then tested its hold against his tugs. He loosed his knife from his belt. The blade felt so tiny in his fist. His knife was nowhere near as large as the one James carried. And it made George's weapon look like a cutlass. It would have to do. All he had to kill El Diablo was the steel in his hand. It was sharp. It would cut through flesh.

It would have to.

Lito called out. He imitated the sounds of an animal in distress. Noises his Abuelo and Tio, his grandfather and uncle, used to lure out their prey when they hunted. Their favorite was the rabbit. It was easiest to vocalize and most recognizable, regardless of region. Rabbits were everywhere. They multiplied and flourished in all kinds of environments. Woods, grasslands, deserts. The only purpose they served was to feed the food chain higher up the ladder. And prey loved the way they tasted.

A foul odor drifted to his nostrils. The smell of rotting flesh and mucky swamp bottoms pierced his nose. His stomach gurgled as it threatened to send back his last meal. Lito's head darted left and right in search of the devil he knew was coming closer. He strained to hear its approach even though he knew El Chupacabra moved silently. His breathing became sporadic and shallow. A sheen of perspiration broke out along his neck and forehead.

Madre de Dios.

Lito whispered prayers as his fear escalated, demanding he leave at once.

Before it was too late.

Lito stopped breathing. The last wisp of air caught in his throat.

Ojos rojo.

The red eyes glowed with fury. Each silent step brought the creature closer. The eyes growing bigger. More intense.

Dread coursed through Lito's veins. He tugged at the rope, trying with all his might to run but it held fast. Lito used his blade to saw through the hemp. It would be useless, taking too long and expending all his energy.

Lito continued sawing anyway.

A low grumble emanated, reverberating through the ground, into his feet and up his legs. Lito's spine locked in terror. He tasted the stench on the back of his tongue.

"El Diablo, no necessito. El Diablo, no necessito."

Lito clenched his eyes shut. He spoke through gritted teeth, anticipating the pain of the first bite.

Something that sounded like laughter gave Lito pause. He opened his eyes to find El Chupacabra staring into his face. Its nose touching his nose. Its foul breath whisking his mustache.

Lito wet himself. The creature must have smelled the urine because it glanced down and grinned.

The beating of El Chupacabra's heart hurt Lito's ears. It was loud and powerful. Yet, slow. As if the creature were calm and gently strolling along a game trail. By contrast, Lito's heart hammered in his chest. He could feel it but he couldn't hear it over the beast's own beat.

Madre de Dios.

Lito swung his arm wide with all his might. The blade sunk into the flesh, all the way to the handle.

El Chupacabra brayed a deafening shriek, its head thrown back against the night. The mighty roar freed what was left in Lito's bladder. He twisted the knife a quarter turn.

And then El Chupacabra struck. The monster tore a chunk from Lito's chest. Shirt, skin and muscle mixed in a lightning flash of pain. El Chupacabra swallowed the meat whole, without chewing, as blood and saliva flew from its fangs.

Lito felt the world turn black. His consciousness wavered as the excruciating anguish of his wounds raced to his brain. Lito tried to get his hand back to the knife but the creature had moved too much for him to find it again. He closed his eyes against the attack, choosing to give in to his inevitable demise. He grew content as death neared, for he had stood up to his demon and had landed a good shot. Even if he hadn't killed El Chupacabra, the monster would leave this one meal with a reminder, a memento of a killing that hadn't gone as smoothly as it should have. And for that, Lito held his head up with pride, offering his tender neck flesh to the devil.

El Chupacabra roared.

It was a roar of surprise and not triumph.

CHAPTER 43

James jabbed his knife into El Chupacabra's back. A gush of hot blood drenched his fist as he tugged the knife free of the monster's flesh. It stood on its hind legs, howling into the coming dawn, in response to the deft stab wound.

He wished he had his pistol. As James ran to the cottonwood tree, he had heard the commotion and had tried to pull the gun from his holster. But it had slipped through his fingers. James knew he had little time to search for the lost weapon in the darkness. He needed to save Lito.

El Chupacabra turned toward James. It bellowed another ear-splitting roar, one with so much might that James' chest vibrated as if he were bouncing around in an unsteady stagecoach along a rocky trail. The creature's noise sounded panicked, unsure. James felt empowered and decided to strike again while the advantage was still his.

The beast dropped down to all fours, its hind legs reared to the sky as its muzzle dipped low to the earth in an aggressive posture. James charged it quickly to get the jump. As he flew through the air with the knife blade poised above his head in a two-handed axe-swing, El Chupacabra flung its bloody snout from left to right, tossing James away like a fly on a horse's tail.

Sailing through the darkness, the world seemed to slow down around James. He heard Lito's gasps for air. The smell of death, like a fetid pile of carrion bait, pierced his nostrils, turning his stomach. The subtle orange-purple of the approaching morning light outlining the blackened horizon, promised a new day, calm and beautiful, oblivious to the horrors that unfolded around him.

Before he could scramble to his feet, El Chupacabra was upon him. The massive jaws snapped and slavered above James. He swatted at the razor-sharp teeth, defending his face against the attacks, but not well enough to avoid slices along his forearm. James brought his knife down hard, jamming the tip of the blade in the creature's snout. A geyser of blood jettisoned into the air, painting James' face in a splatter of crimson.

El Chupacabra shrieked, pulling away. It scratched its mighty claws to free the knife. James rolled to his feet and hurried at the monster. He jumped on its back, wrapping his arms around its neck in an attempt to choke it to death.

His arms never made it all the way around the stout neck.

The beast knocked the blade from its face and bucked James from its back. As he flew across the desert, James wondered how many times he would find himself flying through the air tonight. With no time to answer his own questions, James thudded to the ground and hurried to face the attacking monster.

El Chupacabra growled, diving across an enormous expanse as it flung its body directly into James' path. Both bodies collided in a deafening crunch of bone and meat. James bore the brunt of the collision. His limbs went numb and his head snapped backwards in a whiplash of fury.

He hit the ground. Lifeless.

James was aware of his surroundings but he could do little about his situation. His brain was mired in darkness, scrounging for an opening to crawl back into the world around him. He tried to move his legs, but they wouldn't respond, regardless of how loudly his mind screamed at them to flee.

Deep within his comatose state, James smelled the beast. The noxious fumes bit down through his paralysis, an odor that could overwhelm one hundred outhouses left to fester in the triple-digit summer heat of Texas, with slaughtered pig guts hung from shack to shack and saloon-floor vomit flowing beneath like a babbling brook.

It was that bad.

El Chupacabra drooled into James' face, the sticky wetness puddled in his closed eyelids.

James saw his daddy, the legendary Wyatt Earp. A look of disappointment sagged his features, pulling his iconic mustache toward his boot tips.

Sarah cried out to James, in a different time, her black hair and crystal blue eyes gleaming in the dappled sunlight of a meadow. She held her arms wide to entice James into a loving embrace.

Carson flipped over his cards. His smile grew wide as he watched James' frustration at playing another horrible hand of poker. Carson's lips moved to say James should have paid attention, but no words were audible.

Lito screamed.

James clawed his way through the opaque terror in his soul. He needed to save Lito and his family. But most urgent, James needed to save himself.

His eyes fluttered through the sappy saliva. A murky image of a monster so horrific hung inches from his face.

James swung his head forward. His forehead caught El Chupacabra's mouth. The fangs sliced two long gashes along either side of James' head, almost as wide as his temples. It sent the beast backwards, just far enough for James to will his body to crawl from under the impending attack.

As he stood on shaky legs, El Chupacabra returned with a vengeance. Its eyes glowed red with hostility and malice. James threw his arm up to deflect the attack. The massive jaws clamped down on James' forearm. He felt the bones within give way to the thunderous pressure.

James screamed. He dropped the knife from his right hand as he focused on freeing his arm from the maw of the monster. El Chupacabra gnashed and wrangled, carrying James' body with it like a rag doll.

He swung his fist into the boulder-sized head of the creature. Each punch felt like he had struck an anvil. And did about as much damage as punching an anvil.

James landed on his back, the creature once again upon him in a deadly clutch.

"Let go. Let go of me."

El Chupacabra gripped his arm tighter, crushing bone and muscle within its jaws.

James used his free hand to feel around for his blade. He knew his chances of surviving this battle were fading with each minute. If he couldn't get his hands on a weapon, quickly, then James would succumb to the mighty monster like the previous homeowner.

He wished he hadn't dropped his gun.

James wrenched his mangled arm away from El Chupacabra's mouth. The pain ran like lightning through his brain. His fingers danced along the dirt, working to find his last chance at life.

Where is that knife?

CHAPTER 44

A deafening report cracked through the air. All the noise of the fray ceased, momentarily, as the bullet cut through the dawn and found its mark. El Chupacabra leaped away from James with anguished cry.

James gripped his broken arm and rolled to his belly. A tall shape approached from the east, backlit by the coming morning light. He knew who walked his way before he heard the recognizable sound of tobacco juice skitter along the dust.

George.

The large man cocked the trigger-guard of his repeating rifle, jettisoning the spent cartridge and slamming a fresh bullet into the chamber. He raised the rifle to his shoulder, sighted down the barrel and fired another shot without slowing his pace.

A fleshy thump told George and James that the second round had again found its target.

So did the high-pitched screech of the beast.

George bent to lift James to his feet. As he stood, James swooned from the pain in his crushed arm. He worried about farm chores with a busted up, gimpy appendage. Then he realized farm chores wouldn't matter if he didn't live through this fight.

"Can you fight?"

James winced. He nodded to George. "I'm gonna try."

"Let's send it back to Hell." George began to smirk when his body went flying.

Blinking against the speed of action, James watched as El Chupacabra tackled George.

The rifle went flying.

He hurried to get the gun and save George. James lifted the rifle to his shoulder before realizing his broken arm would provide no support for the barrel. He would have to fire the gun from his hip, one-handed, and hope for the best.

I hope this thing doesn't tear my other arm off with its kick.

James swung the rifle in a circle, cocking the trigger-guard as gravity brought it back around. He pulled the trigger and the gun bucked.

His shot flew wide.

James gritted his teeth against the pain. The rifle was useless in his hands and the kick sent shockwaves through his body as its vibration reached his broken arm.

He dropped the gun.

As he shifted his attention back to George, El Chupacabra charged at James. He only had time enough to notice one glowing orb in the beast's head before it slammed into him at full speed. James slid along the earth, on his back, for what seemed an eternity. The whole time, El Chupacabra continued to run at him with its slavering mouth hung wide and fangs stretched forward.

It snapped at his boot, a long blade chomping through his foot. James screamed as a fresh wound messaged his brain. He immediately curled his leg into his chest, an autonomic response to the bite. His knee caught the monster in the face. But the misdirection was momentary as it dove forward to strike James again.

The bloody mouth lurched at his throat. James started to roll to his side, attempting to avoid the attack, when El Chupacabra pawed his body back into place like newborn kitten. The monster had been so much bigger and stronger than James had ever imagined. It dwarfed other dog-like animals such as coyotes and wolves. James couldn't help but compare El Chupacabra's size to his old friend Crouching Bear... when he turned into the animal.

CRACK!

James got crushed by the dead weight that collapsed onto his chest. His air expelled from his lungs, forced away by the immense body of El Chupacabra. It fell on him as George swung the barrel end of the repeating rifle. The hickory handle connected with the beast's skull again and again.

He used his wobbly legs to lift the creature just enough so he could roll out from under it before it collapsed again. The weight of its thud kicked up a bonfire's worth of smoky dust. James gagged as he swallowed the particles, trying to fill his lungs back up.

CRACK!

George kept up the swinging. He landed strike after strike, knocking El Chupacabra senseless. The monster exhaled an enormous breath as it fell to the blows. Relief washed over James as the beast slumped into the earth. The battle was over.

Just as quickly, the pain of all his injuries surfaced, reminding James he would have been better off dead than living through his wounds.

I'm still alive.

James sat up. He cradled his broken arm against his chest as it continued to heave and gasp for more air. George bent to rest the rifle barrel across his knees. He'd gassed himself from swinging the gun multiple times with all his might.

He couldn't remember ever being happier to see George. James felt a bit guilty over his treatment of the man. Had it been childish jealousy over the man's romantic interest in his mother? Or did he abhor having to fend off the challenge of an alpha male at home? A place where James had promised HE would be the leader and provider?

George cleared the leafy chew from his gums. He spat the remainder of saliva and knelt next to James.

"You're welcome."

James flushed. His dander raised as the thought of needing George to protect him like a father figure squirmed under his skin.

I'm not going to call him Daddy.

"Thanks. And we're even, by the way."

"Not according to my ledger."

James held his hand out, prompting George to help lift him to his feet. The bigger man pulled James up like a man lifting a child.

You're not my Daddy.

"Have you forgotten Crouching Bear?"

George chuckled. "Ain't you that saved me. That medicine man brought me back to life."

James bit the inside of his cheek. He wanted to punch George in the mouth but he knew it would be fruitless fighting with one arm.

"I'm the one who got you there and got you home."

The silence between them hung in the air as they agreed to disagree. James hobbled on his bloody foot.

"Let's help Lito before it's too late."

George slung his arm around James' shoulder to assist in the walk toward the cottonwood tree. As they shuffled slowly along, James became aware of the soft whimpering coming from the spot where Lito rested. He cheered up at the sound, knowing if Lito could make noise then, at least, he was still alive.

They found Lito huddled in a bloody heap, crying and twisted with his tied arm wrenched behind his back.

But he was alive.

CHAPTER 45

James slumped to his knees. He used his good arm to lift Lito's head from the ground. Lito choked up some blood. He tried to force a smile but it was quickly wiped away by another fit of coughing.

"James..."

"I'm right here, amigo. I'm right here." James was concerned for Lito's condition and he wanted to help the man. He just wasn't sure moving Lito would be the best choice at the moment.

"El Diablo..."

James nodded. "We got him. He won't be killing anymore."

George mumbled into James' ear. "Think he'll make it?"

"Of course he'll make it." James snapped at George. He couldn't understand why he would talk like that in front of a dying man. Where George was practical, James sowed seeds of hope.

"Let's get him back to the ranch. Make him comfortable." James looked around. He recalled George had walked here, and his hopes of transporting Lito back to the house on horseback fizzled.

George barked. He dropped to the ground, clutching the back of his legs.

El Chupacabra snorted, spraying bloody snot at the cluster of men.

James dropped Lito's head and scrambled to his feet. By the time he stood up, the beast was on him. It tore a hunk of meat from the dangling broken arm. James screamed, sounding shrill like a little girl. He yanked his arm back as he could feel sinew and tendon rip from his wound. The monster swatted a bloody paw across James' face. The scratches left tracks under his hairline and sent his head backwards.

George shouted at El Chupacabra. He shucked his blade free of its sheath, tossing the knife from hand to hand as if he wanted to tease the creature. George ran at the animal. Just as he neared the beast, George spun around and feinted a parry. Using his opposite hand, George swung the blade upward, impaling the throat of El Chupacabra.

A fresh spray of crimson showered George. He blinked away the dark coating around his eyes.

James charged with his knife in his hand. It felt strange to run with one hand flopping dead at his side. He tried to ignore the awkward feeling so he could concentrate on the task at hand. James skewered El Chupacabra behind the front right shoulder. The mighty devil rose to its hind legs and threw itself at James. He managed to hobble aside in the nick of time. But the left paw swiped at his feet and tripped him up.

George dove onto the creature. He jabbed his blade at El Chupacabra's head and missed. Instead, the knife found purchase behind the animal, lower down the back of its neck. It threw its head back, tossing George aside as easily as clean laundry sways in the afternoon breeze.

James saw the rifle in the dirt. He glanced back at El Chupacabra. It had caught his attention and seemed to figure out his next move. The monster shifted itself between James and the rifle. He had to get a hold of the gun if they were to defeat the devil. Knives only angered the beast and bludgeoning it was like hammering away at a pile of rocks with a dull mallet.

They'd need to shoot it.

He ran in a semi-circle around El Chupacabra, the beast's eyes following him as he trekked around. James hoped to slide under the animal in order to avoid being swatted while scooping up the weapon. As James tucked his head down and ducked the swatting motion, he missed the rifle as his body skimmed past.

El Chupacabra didn't waste time. It pounced at James and shoved its muzzle hard into James' back. The air whizzed out of his lungs, and he folded in half under the weight of the creature. It snapped its fangs around his head, missing by a few hairs each time James swung his arms to protect himself.

The force of a gunshot close to his face blew gunpowder into James' eyes.

El Chupacabra spun to face the smoking barrel of George's rifle. He hurried to load another bullet but he wasn't quick enough. The animal bit at George and both bodies tumbled to the earth in a cloud of dust.

James shook the cobwebs from his mind. He gulped a few gusts of air and crawled on one hand toward the battle that raged ahead. James heard George's knife slice into meat several times. And he heard El Chupacabra ripping flesh in its fangs as it complained about the stab wounds.

He had to get in there fast to help George.

James picked up the rifle. He checked the chamber to see if another round had been loaded.

A copper shell stood half-way out of the feeder. George had nearly finished loading the rifle for another shot. But he hadn't completed the job.

James shoved the bullet in until it clicked into place. He cocked the hammer and jammed the barrel into the back of monster's head. He pulled the trigger.

The bang threw James backwards as he used his hip to keep the gun steady.

The bullet pulverized the skull of El Chupacabra. Fluids of different colors and consistency rained down on them as James dropped to the ground. He choked to get more air into his lungs, inhaling mists of carnage with each breath.

George lie prone, not moving. James tried to speak to George, to reassure him that the monster was dead. But only grunts and squeaks crept past his lips. James used what little strength he had left to drag himself to George, one fingernail at a time. The process was slow and painful.

He stretched his face over George's mouth to see if he could distinguish any breathing. As he strained to listen for air, an avalanche of sound erupted behind James. He rolled to seek the cause of the new commotion.

El Chupacabra, with three-quarters of its head missing, reared up with a last gasp of killing in its soul. The sole red orb, still glowing in its socket, had dimmed to an ember in brightness and size. The sound that came from the remainder of the beast's throat was more horrific than the image that rose above James.

He shielded his head against the next wave of attacks, only to see the light fade in the monster's eye. The colossal remains fell to the ground with a croak and a new plume of blood.

CHAPTER 46

The noxious smell of the slaughtered beast lifted the bile in James' stomach. He bent and vomited like he had never done so before. Using the back of his sleeve, James cleared his lips and stood straight. He admired the rays of sunlight that peaked above the horizon, casting shadows along the scene of devastation. James felt awestruck by God's grace of such a beautiful moment after a night of such evil and carnage.

James stumbled toward George. The man's face was covered in blood. The sight stunned James as he attempted to figure out how to explain to his mother why his face would never be the same. He crouched next to George and checked for breathing.

"You gonna kiss me or something?"

James retreated with surprise. Inside, he was elated George was alive enough to continue busting his chops. Outwardly, James wanted to remain stoic and manly.

"I wouldn't kiss you with El Chupacabra's lips."

They both chuckled weakly.

"Your pretty face has seen better days, that's for sure." James tried to use humor to convey the damage he saw.

"Get me some chew, will ya?"

James rummaged around in George's pockets. His dungarees were torn and soaked in blood. The soggy clothes made the search more difficult. And James only had one hand to do it. He found the wet clump of tobacco leaves in a mangled wrap. James unfurled the wrapper, shook some of the excess fluids from the plant and began to bring the wad to George's lips.

"Ain'tcha gonna clear away this muck so I can chew?"

"I don't want to hurt you."

George winced and grunted. "Ain't nothing wrong with my face. It's just blood from that dang blasted creature."

Relieved, James used his damp sleeve to swab away the gore that covered George's face. He shoved the wad of leaf into George's front teeth. His tongue scooped the remains of the chew and neatly tucked it into his cheek. James shook his head in disgust.

"Can you move?"

George chewed in silence with his eyes closed. He attempted to raise himself before lowering back to the ground.

"My damn back is seized up. I'll be alright in a few minutes, I reckon."

James sat down to relieve his knees. He began to think about Carson and wanted to get back to the ranch to check on his well-being. Carson would require a lot of healing. They all would. The move to Texas had done more than physical damage to the family. His mother was extremely sore at him. Carson would be devastated as he had nearly lost his life yet again. And James had much more to consider about how to provide for his loved ones. Could he manage to do the right thing? Would he convince them all to forgive him? How would he handle the curse of his paternal bloodline?

Then there was George.

"I want you to know..." James choked up a little. He stopped himself before he broke out into a balling fit like a little kid. He forced his eyes to the sunrise so he could hide the tears that welled up. "I want you to know how sorry I am."

George rolled his head to the side and spat. He returned his attention to James. "Is this the part where you're gonna kiss me?"

They both laughed.

"I shoulda been nicer to you. You always save my hide and yet I resented you tracking us down."

George said nothing.

"I guess, I've never seen my mother behave like she did. It's always been her and me. And more recently, Carson." James tossed a pebble. "I'm not used to having another man around."

George sat up with groans and winces. James helped lift him up.

"I ain't your daddy, if that's what you're worried about."

James tossed another stone.

"You know..." George moved the chaw from one cheek to the other. "All my life, I've been a loner. My momma died when I was a kid. My pappy was a mean drunk, always beatin' on me and leaving me to fend for myself for days at a time. I reckon I got used to being alone and only countin' on myself."

James nodded.

"Then ya'll took care of me. I didn't know what to make of it all." George tried to lift his wounded leg. The pain was too much so he lowered it again. "When you moved away, something was missing. Like I lost something that was important to me."

"Is this the part where you kiss me?" James slapped George's shoulder in jest. George glared at James.

"Sorry."

"Anyway, I realized I never had no family but you guys was the closest thing. I figured I could settle down and quit fighting and being a mean bastard. Maybe enjoy life for a change." George looked away. "That's why I came after you guys."

"I thought you came for my mother."

George nodded. "I did. Mostly for her. But you and Carson are okay too." He slugged James in the shoulder, knocking him over. James landed on his broken arm and howled at the shooting pain.

James thought of striking back at George until he saw the wide grin along the man's face. James broke into laughter. George just nodded.

"Let's get back to the ranch and get cleaned up. See how Carson is doing."

James hobbled over to George. He used every fiber in his being to help lift the large man to his feet. Both men used each other as crutches to stay on their feet.

"Let's get Lito first."

"Ain't that wetback done enough already?"

James pursed his lips. He wished George would ease up on the attitude but he knew it would take a lot of time and effort to change George's ways.

"Yes, he has. That's why I'm going to get him."

Shuffling slowly, the men worked their way around the gory remains of El Chupacabra toward Lito. James avoided looking at the mess, choosing to put the image of the monster behind him. He'd seen enough blood and tragedy in his short life and he had no intentions of adding more clutter to his nightmares.

CHAPTER 47

Lito lay in a pool of his own blood. The scene was as grisly as anything James had ever witnessed before. Possibly more so because of his friend. James swallowed hard and hurried the last few steps to Lito on his own.

James didn't know where to begin. He didn't want to immerse himself in more blood and filth, but he had to attend to Lito so he would have to suck it up and deal with the disgusting task. He gingerly neared Lito and checked to see if the man was breathing. James felt the slightest air escaping past Lito's lips. James whispered to him.

"Lito. Lito."

A raspy groan, so weak and frail, barely audible, returned.

"Lito. It's James."

"James?" The question arrived as a croak.

"Help me sit him up." James beseeched George for assistance. A gentle hand on James' broken arm brought his attention back to Lito.

"No, mi amigo."

James searched Lito's face. His eyes gazed upward, blank and distant. Unable to focus.

"I'm here. I want to get you some help."

Lito smiled briefly. It cleared away with a fit of choking.

"Muerto."

James shot a glance at George. George shrugged. "I don't understand that gibberish."

Lito's dry tongue grazed his bloody lips. His eyes rolled slowly back. James shook him.

"Stay with me, buddy. Don't go. We'll get you help."

"No necessito. Por favor."

George grumbled and spat.

"El...El Chupacabra. He gone?"

James nodded. "Yes, we killed him."

"Bueno. Bueno."

"Why did you do it? Why didn't you wait for us?" James fought back some tears. He managed to keep his voice steady.

"Ees my fault."

"It wasn't your fault. You didn't do anything wrong."

Lito nodded once. "I...I didn't help rapido."

James grew frustrated with Lito's words. Both the content and the delivery, bouncing between English and Spanish.

"Ees okay. Su familia es..." Another fit of choking cut into Lito's thoughts.

"What can I do? Do you need water? Tell me what to do." James' voice quavered with emotion.

"Gracias. Just...say...gracias."

Tears fell from his eyes. James blinked a fresh batch away as he watched Lito drift slowly across to the other side.

"Gracias." James whimpered. "Gracias, amigo."

Lito smiled. For the first time since James had arrived, Lito's eyes showed clarity and recognition.

"The nino. Take care of el nino."

James nodded as Lito's last breath escaped. His eyes clouded over and glared above towards the heavens. James gently laid Lito down and closed the man's eyelids. He sniffled and sobbed. James' legacy for getting people killed lived on. Pangs of guilt and sorrow filled his chest.

"Suppose we oughta bury him." George's voice resembled James'. It was slightly shaky, as if the big man had also been touched by Lito's passing.

Maybe he has a soft side after all.

James rose to his feet. He shambled over to George.

"I know the perfect spot."

He gathered stones in the general vicinity and placed them on top of Lito's body. They'd have to come back with shovels to bury the man. Until then, they would cover him up with stones so the wildlife wouldn't pick away at the corpse. It would also slow the decaying process since the body would remain in the hot sun until they could put it in the ground.

They finished covering Lito and began to make their way back to the ranch. A gentle morning breeze had relieved them of their sweaty skin and promised a gorgeous day ahead. Once again, James found himself contemplating the irony of God's beauty juxtaposed against the evil nature of mankind and the violence run amok in the world. He supposed he finally understood why all the preachers contended that the afterlife was something worth working towards. Because living was a struggle. It was dirty and dangerous. And painful on so many levels.

George chastised James for not helping him sooner. He pointed out the various wounds inflicted by El Chupacabra and how they could have been avoided if James had gotten to work sooner. James listened with humor in his heart even though he knew he could have done better. The whole battle shouldn't have happened the way it did. If only he had done his duty when he had had his chance.

Carson would be safe.

George would be healthy.

His mother would be happy.

Lito would still be alive.

James realized he'd have more demons to live with now that another chapter in his life had ended. He needed to figure out their future. Would they stay in Texas? Would they move on, take their chances in a new place? What if they encountered new dangers? What if there were more evils awaiting them here on the farm?

His heard pounded with all the thoughts and worries. James wished he had grown up differently. He imagined a normal life on a homestead somewhere back in Iowa. A regular family life with his mother...and a father. Someone other than Wyatt Earp. A man he could have worshipped for being a stout hardworking family man.

Instead, James chased the ghost of a legend. An impossible ideal, most likely more fantasy than reality. His gut churned with the choices he had made and the wrongs those choices had created. There was so much hurt left behind in its wake.

George shook James' shoulder. "I said, I hope you don't mind me asking your mother to marry me."

James blinked himself back to the present. "Wait. What?"

"Boy, have you heard a damned word I said this whole time? I want to do right by your mother. Take care of her. Make her mine and keep her safe from all of your shenanigans."

"You really think my mother would go for that? You're too...filthy and unrefined."

"I can bathe once in a while."

James snorted. "It'll cost you more than a few baths. Wait till she gives you grief for the cussing and table manners."

George spat.

"Don't even get me started on the tobacco."

George grimaced.

"The least you can do is put in a good word for me. After all the times I've saved yer tail..."

James laughed. George joined him.

"I can put in all the good words you want. The rest is up to you." James stopped in his tracks. "But I ain't calling you daddy. Ever."

George needled James. "Sounds like a righteous plan, son."

CHAPTER 48

Sarah had been worried about James and George all night. She silently prayed they would come home safely. They had left in a rush to find Lito and she knew they would continue searching until they found him. Dead or alive.

But Sarah had been busy herself. Keeping Carson alive. The boy had suffered some atrocious wounds to his neck and limbs. He'd lost lots of blood. Sarah had worked the whole night, applying bandages and poultices, changing them every half hour or so to keep the wounds dressed in fresh linens. She fed the boy broth and warm water, forcing it past his lips so that his body could fight off infection and build its strength while his wounds mended.

Speaking of mending, Sarah toiled to sew up the bites. She had been happy she had the extra threads and needles from the dress making shop. The supplies had come in handy as Sarah fed the odd assortment of colored strings through Carson's tender flesh, tightening the gaping holes so the healing could begin, and to stave off contaminants.

Sarah had never been one to have a strong stomach, especially when it came to blood and such. However, saving people she cared about trumped any nausea that could be brought on by such tasks. She ignored her own bodily functions in order to care for Carson. Her bladder felt as if it swollen to the size of a watermelon in her abdomen. She was dying to relieve herself but she feared stepping out for even a minute.

The door kicked in. Sarah heard the slow shuffle-calumph of dusty boots in the kitchen. She kissed Carson's sweaty forehead and rushed to see if the men had arrived. Or if she would need to fight off someone else. Or something.

Sarah rounded the corner and found the blood-soaked men holding each other up. James and George looked as if they had lost a fight with a cornered kitty. Except the cat would have had to have been the size of a stallion.

"My goodness. Look at you." Sarah's eyes misted. She covered her mouth to stifle a scream or a cry. Perhaps both.

James tugged back one of the chairs from the table. He slumped into it in slow motion, wincing the whole way down. George teetered and used the chair backs to walk himself around to Sarah. He held onto her shoulders, his arms shaking. Sarah squeezed him tight until he groaned. She realized she had most likely put pressure on one of his wounds. Sarah apologized and gently set George down on a three-legged stool.

"How is Carson?" James' eyes sagged with exhaustion.

Sarah rushed over to him. She quickly checked his face and head, scouring all the cuts and abrasions. "He's healing as best he can." She traced two slash marks that ran up from each of James' temples. He winced and backed away. Sarah apologized again. She got a few more towels from the kitchen and began tearing off sections. She dunked each section into the water barrel and then dabbed at James' cuts.

James pushed away her hands. "Go help HIM. I'm fine. Except for my busted arm."

Sarah bit her lip. She noticed the odd angle at which his forearm dangled.

George countered. "I'm a man. I can handle the pain. Best take care of yer little boy."

Sarah put her hands on her hips. "Now, don't the two of you think you can just waltz right in here and carry on like two little devils. I'm tired and I'm fixing to burst from having to pee so bad. If I wasn't exhausted, I would tan both your bottoms and put you outside in the heat."

DESERT FANGS

James and George blinked against her tirade.

"Now," Sarah straightened her skirt, "I must excuse myself for a moment. And when I return, I expect to find both of you cleaning yourselves up." Sarah pointed at George. "And I mean with soap, Mister." She tucked a flyaway strand of dark hair behind her ear. "You'll need to clean those cuts and then we'll see to patching you up right away. We've got plenty of chores to do around here."

James clucked his tongue. "Aren't you going to ask us about El Chupacabra?"

Sarah knew the monster was dead. Their condition and the length of time they had been gone provided her with a lucky guess as to the fate of the beast. Besides, she knew if the creature was still alive, James and George would have shown more signs of tension and fear. Instead, they revealed their relief in the casual demeanor they both displayed as they sat in those chairs. Exhausted and resolute. She was smart enough to know the answer.

"You can tell me all about your little adventure when we eat supper. Until then, I want to see cleanliness and elbow grease. Nobody has time to lollygag around."

George grumbled under his breath.

"You have something to say, young man?"

George averted his eyes and shook his head.

"Good. I'll be back in a few minutes and we'll get you both fixed up and fed."

Sarah rushed out the door to the outhouse. She feared she wouldn't make it and thought seriously about hiking up her skirt and watering the dirt where she stood. But it wouldn't be very lady-like. Sarah pulled the door of the outhouse closed and set to do her business. As she rested for the first time in hours, Sarah began to shake and cry. She had kept up a facade of bravery all night but her emotions needed to release the strain as badly as her bladder needed to empty.

She wrapped her arms across her chest and held tight. The tears were as much for joy and relief as they were for sorrow at all they had gone through since leaving Iowa. With each passing day, Sarah grew tired. A constant schedule of cooking and cleaning and working were difficult alone. But taking care of three boys made it even harder. She chuckled to herself as she admitted that the older the boys got, the more caretaking they required.

Sarah loved James and Carson. She would lay her life down for them without question. She tried to figure out if she had more room to add another one. George was big in stature.

And he would require his size in caretaking just to get his table manners up to snuff.

CHAPTER 49

After several days of cleanup and rest, James started to feel more like himself. Except for his broken arm. Sarah had used crude fragments of wood to create a splint for his arm. She'd taken a trip into town to pick up some tonics and elixirs to speed along their recovery. And she summoned Doc Winters to come out to the farm. The doctor fixed up James and George with proper stitching and braces. He'd also looked after Carson. The doctor's concern for the boy was so strong he volunteered to stay by Carson's bedside for the night. He implored the others to get a solid night's rest while he kept vigil over the boy.

The healing process would be slow but it had begun once they had buried Lito under the old cottonwood tree and fixed a rudimentary crucifix to mark the site. James promised to return once he was healed so he could erect a more permanent monument to commemorate the memory of their fallen friend.

Doc Winters mopped his brow and advised the family on Carson's care. He insisted they remain vigilant. The doctor believed Carson would survive but he wasn't out of the woods yet. He'd lost too much blood and suffered nearly fatal injuries. He commended Sarah on her dressings and treatment, confirming Carson would be dead if she hadn't cleaned the wounds and fed his body to keep up his strength.

She thanked the doctor and saw him to his horse.

It would be another week of round the clock care before Carson would come out of his comatose state.

Carson's eyes fluttered. He squinted against the light as he tried to adjust to the brightness. James teared up.

"Carson?"

The boy took in his surroundings without moving his head. James could tell Carson was still too weak to move. He called out to his mother and George to come see Carson now that he was awake.

"Hi, baby. How do you feel?" Sarah pushed in closer, almost toppling James from the stool.

"What happened to your arm?"

James glanced down at his sling. "Aw, this? Nothing much. It's good to see you again."

Carson blinked, his eyes shifting between their faces. He tried to sit up but Sarah pushed him back down gently.

"Take it easy. You've had a full...day."

James shot his mother a look. He realized she didn't want to concern Carson with the truth so soon after recovering. There would be plenty of time to recount the tale of El Chupacabra. Pretending he had only been asleep for a few hours would make more sense to the boy.

"Are you hungry? I have some soup for you."

Carson nodded slowly. Sarah kissed his forehead and rushed back to the kitchen.

James brushed Carson's sweaty hair aside. He wished Carson had been spared so much trauma. James believed he should have been the one to nearly die, not an innocent little boy like Carson.

"The Screeper..."

James glanced over his shoulder. He listened for his mother's whereabouts. Feeling safe, James figured it would be wise to let Carson know about the monster. "No more Screeper."

Carson smiled weakly.

"You don't have to be scared of what's out there anymore."

"Where's George?"

James snickered. "He's keeping Sarah company in the kitchen. It's been a little difficult for him to get around lately."

DESERT FANGS

Carson closed his eyes. His lips curled in a lazy yawn that tugged at James' heart strings.

"Lito?"

James froze. He scrambled through different excuses for why Lito was no longer around. James knew they'd have to come clean about the man's death eventually. But now wouldn't be a good time to upset Carson.

"He's...uh...in the fields." James blushed with the awkward choice of words. He wasn't lying but the reality was too close for his comfort.

Carson broke wind. A temporary smirk lit his face. James chuckled. "Well, it sounds like you're back to your old self."

The boy's grin grew wider. James began to match the mirth on Carson's face until he got his first whiff of recovery gas.

"Oh, God. That's awful." James waved his good arm in front of his face to get fresh air.

Carson chuckled.

"Soup is on." Sarah brought a small tray with a piping hot bowl of soup and a small piece of bread. She stopped in her tracks a few feet from the bed. "What is that...smell?" She quickly placed the tray down and held her sleeve to her nose.

Carson's laughter increased. James caught the contagion and started laughing at his mother's expense, even though he struggled to breathe through the fog himself.

James pointed at Carson. "It wasn't me. He did it."

Sarah crossed her arms. "James, do you expect me to believe all that odor can come from a small boy like him. God doesn't approve of liars."

"I'm not lying." James protested loudly, realizing the more he pleaded his case, the more guilty he would look.

Carson enjoyed every second. His laughter rolled from his lungs to his belly, sounding more like the Carson of old.

Sarah wrinkled her nose. "Okay, stinky. You feed him then while I go for some fresh air." She raised the window another inch and then hustled to leave the room.

James shook his head. He felt much better knowing Carson was coming around. The relief was palpable, and James sensed Sarah's lighter mood since Carson had woken. He moved the tray closer and spooned in a generous portion of broth. James blew on it a couple times to cool it just enough to pass Carson's lips. The boy gulped it down and appeared to get hungrier with each spoonful. After eating in silence for several minutes, Carson questioned James.

"James?"

"Yeah, buddy."

"How did you get rid of the Screeper?"

James thought about his response for a moment. He decided the truth made more sense than telling stories. But he had a story ready to go, just the same.

"While you were sleeping, George carried you outside. When the Screeper charged us, George pointed your butt at him and the monster died after one whiff."

Carson's face sunk. The fear etched deep along his brow as he contemplated the proximity to the beast.

James cracked up, and his laughter exploded as Carson's expression remained horrified.

CHAPTER 50

James watched the azure sky meld into a mandarin sunset. A refreshing breeze displaced a bramble of tumbleweeds along the arid soil. After all they had been through, a quiet moment sitting alone on the porch was a welcome treat.

He rocked his chair gently, forcing the plank behind him to creak like an old man's joints. James adjusted his damaged arm across his chest. The pain had become increasingly less sharp and had settled into more of a dull throbbing irritation.

The door swung open.

Sarah stepped onto the porch and took a deep breath. She tightened the bun that fastened her hair and rubbed her hands together.

"Mind if I sit down, young man?"

James snickered. "Not at all, ma'am."

He started to rise as if he would help her sit but Sarah waved him off.

They sat for a long while in silence. Both lost in their thoughts and taking in the serenity of the landscape.

"I spoke to George." James glanced at Sarah to gauge her reaction. He was disappointed that she remained expressionless.

Sarah said nothing.

"No guess as to what we spoke about?"

Sarah smirked as she kept her gaze far away. "A woman doesn't need to guess when she's surrounded by men."

James ignored the insult. He didn't altogether disagree with his mother. Men were very simple. Women were extremely complicated.

"He has plans for you." James scratched at his temple. "Sounds like serious plans."

"Is that so?" Sarah finally faced James. "I've got some plans of my own."

James decided to play along with his mother's coy attitude. "Oh, I'm sure you do. Like, "George, get those elbows off the table." And, "George, no spitting in my house." Oh, and my favorite, "George, you march right into that kitchen and take a bath.""

James changed his voice to a mock falsetto as he attempted to imitate his mother. Sarah laughed aloud.

The laughter wound down and another air of silence settled between them.

"Wouldn't you like to know my opinion on the matter?"

Sarah raised her eyebrows. "Regardless of your opinion, I know what I'm going to do."

James nodded. He rocked his chair to hide his nervousness.

"I approve of the relationship." He stopped rocking and stared at Sarah. "Regardless of your opinion."

Sarah placed her hand gently on James' hand. "I'm glad you approve."

After a few minutes of peaceful silence, Sarah stroked James' hand. "Have you decided what we should do with this place? Carson?"

James thought for a moment before responding. "I haven't decided yet."

"I want to stay here. With George. I don't particularly like Texas but I've grown tired of moving." Sarah sighed. "Running."

The admission cut James deeply. He couldn't help feeling responsible for his mother's weariness and frustration. It had always been James who had dictated the moves. He wondered why she had gone along with his ill-fated restlessness. It had never dawned on him to ask her what she thought would be best. James just decided and then she followed.

He regretted his reckless behavior.

"I'm sorry about all this."

Sarah rubbed his neck, ironing out some kinks of tension.

"You're still my baby. You'll always be my baby, James. Someday, when you become a father, you'll understand the undying love and acceptance of your children."

Sarah stomped her foot on the porch boards. The sudden noise shook James from his contemplation.

"Unless you end up like your father."

James grimaced at the barb.

"I'll sleep on it and see how I feel tomorrow." James returned to rocking. "And I'll speak with Carson. I reckon he's got to have his own say one of these days. Now seems like a good time to start."

Sarah rose to her feet. She hugged herself against a slight nip in the air, a chill not typically felt since they'd been in Texas.

"You're growing into a fine young man, James. I don't think you would have thought of Carson's feelings a year ago. I'm proud of you."

She bent to kiss his forehead. She rubbed away a bit of moisture she had left behind. James smiled up at her. Sarah started to go back into the house. As she pulled open the door, James threw in an additional thought.

"I'm not calling him daddy."

Sarah lost herself in a fit of laughter. She closed the door behind her, the traces of her laughs still audible from the porch.

James shook his head.

He had so much to consider and in a short amount of time. Not that anybody had put a timer on his decision. But James felt he owed it to the others to finalize his plan. They'd all been through so much already. Keeping them waiting on his whims wouldn't be fair. His decision would affect their homestead lifestyle.

Should I stay?

If I leave, how will they take care of the animals? The chores? Could George handle it on his own? Would Sarah earn enough from the dress maker to hire a farmhand?

The decision weighed on James like a hundred-pound bag of seed. And the more he focused on it, the harder the decision seemed.

He'd have to rely on the only thing he had ever relied on.

His gut.

James slowly rose, supporting his arm, and inhaled a deep breath of night air. He figured getting to bed early would provide him with a solid night's rest. And, if he was lucky, his subconscious would iron out the details of his plan for him. In the morning, he'd sit with Carson and finalize the plan.

If he decided to leave.

There'd be no point in consulting with his little buddy if he decided to stay on the farm.

As James entered the house, he recalled a more innocent time in his life when he and Carson would dream of adventures from the safety of their small room. Doing chores and playing cards. Camping in their secret hideouts. Avoiding the adults with their seemingly busy lives.

Living for tomorrow. A tomorrow that was always what they had dreamed of. Always something to look forward to.

Things had definitely changed.

Become more serious.

Required more work. More effort.

And tomorrow could be dangerous. Deadly. If they weren't careful.

Things had changed.

James wondered what the future had in store for him.

CHAPTER 51

James had slept in, partly because he had been so tired and partly because he had wanted to give Carson ample time to rise on his own. He listened for Carson's stretch and yawn, a daily signal of his awakening. James heard Carson's yawn. As he rolled over, James notice Carson's stiff motions. The boy remained in a weakened state.

Sitting up, James made eye contact with Carson.

"Good morning, buddy."

"Good morning, James."

James awkwardly crawled over to the bed, careful not to harm his broken arm.

"How are you feeling?" James patted the blanket where Carson's leg hid.

Carson stared at the ceiling as if he had to think about his condition. Or perhaps to test his limbs.

"I still hurted all over."

James smiled. "I'm sorry, pal. The pain will go away eventually."

Carson's expression darkened, taking on a serious tone.

"Are we leavinged this place?"

"I need to talk to you about that."

"I don't want to keep moving. I get hurted every place we go."

James pursed his lips. The conversation had started off on the right foot. But it had taken a sudden turn. He tried to be careful with his words so he wouldn't upset Carson. James hoped to get his point across in a way the boy could understand.

And it broke James' heart to have to leave Carson behind.

"I feel just like you, Carson. Tired. Scared. Hurt." He rubbed his temple as a headache injected itself into his day. "But I can't say the settling down life is for me. I want to settle down. But I can't."

Carson turned his head to the wall. James' belly sank as he felt the disappointment in his best friend's posture.

"I'm sorry. You'll be in good hands with mother and George." James sniffled. "I'll be back. Someday. I have to find whatever it is I've been looking for."

Carson glared over his shoulder at James.

"You're leavinged me." He began to whimper. Carson rubbed his nose with the blanket.

James bit his lip. He searched for the proper words to appease Carson. The sound of Carson's crying chewed through his soul. He thought, for a moment, of throwing away his plan just so he could make Carson happy. Until he realized it would be a death sentence for himself. James would make his mother and Carson happy, but at what cost? He'd climb the walls, always thinking about the what-ifs, and scanning the horizon for that next adventure.

He hated his selfish nature. James wished he could be something else.

Maybe his mother had prophesized it the prior night.

James was destined to be like his father. A man drawn to trouble and hell-may-come. A restless spirit with a need to stretch as far as the west would allow him to go.

He felt as if he were running toward his fate. Willingly.

"I'm sorry, Carson. I love you, buddy. I won't forget you. You know I'll think about you every day of my life."

Carson rolled toward James. His bloodshot eyes blinked a fresh trail of tears.

"I'm going with you, James."

James shook his head. "Don't be silly, Carson. It'll be too dangerous."

"I changed my mind. You can't make me."

"But you love it here. You love the animals and the rocks. And all that land to run around. You love it."

Carson shook his head vehemently. "I love YOU, James."

Tears filled James' eyes. His heart swelled in his chest. The feeling was mutual between the companions. He dabbed at the streaks on his face.

"You know what, buddy? I HAVE paid attention. Just like you've always teased me. And I can see that my place is here. On the farm. With you."

Carson strained to sit up. He lifted himself on one elbow.

"But...we said we would go on adventures. You said we would fight the bad mans."

"We did, Carson. And we won. Now it's time to settle down."

James couldn't believe the words coming from his own mouth. He had intended to strike out across the country and now he found himself tucking his head into a shell like a turtle so his best friend wouldn't get hurt. Hurt more than he'd already suffered.

"But...what if somebody'd else needs us? What if there's another Screeper, James?"

For the first time in his life, James found himself absolutely speechless. He couldn't summon a defense to the points Carson raised.

Or he didn't want to defend it. Carson had come around. And faced the direction James wanted.

"I don't know. You have to be sure about this. Because once we go out there, it will be too far for us to turn back. Well, I mean, right away. We'll come back to mother and George. But we would have to go west first. Are you sure you are okay with that? You won't be scared?"

Carson lowered himself down. He stared at the ceiling for a moment and then locked eyes with James.

"I'm sure. I want to be with you." Carson wiped his runny nose with the back of his hand. "And somebody'd needs us. Right?"

James nodded. He knew what he had to do. It was his calling. And Carson understood it too. James just hoped he could protect Carson from getting hurt in the future. Their adventures to date had been painful for the little guy.

"Right. There's evil out there. Bad people. And we're gonna teach them a lesson."

Carson smiled.

"You know what the most difficult part of our adventure will be?"

Carson shook his head.

"Telling mother that we're both leaving. She is NOT going to be happy."

James mussed Carson's hair.

"I'll call her in here so YOU can tell her the news."

Carson pulled the blanket up over his face. He whispered, "Nooooooo."

James laughed.

Even with all the changes they had gone through, James knew it would be like old times.

The world had another Earp to deal with.

ABOUT THE AUTHOR

Chuck Buda explores the darkest aspects of the human condition. Then he captures its essence for fictional use. He writes during the day and wanders aimlessly all night…alone.

Chuck Buda co-hosts The Mando Method Podcast on Project Entertainment Network with author, Armand Rosamilia. They talk about all aspects of writing. Subscribe so you don't miss an episode. You can find The Mando Method Podcast on iTunes, Stitcher and most other places where podcasts are available. Or you can listen directly from the Project Entertainment Network website.

www.PROJECTENTERTAINMENTNETWORK.com

CPSIA information can be obtained
at www.ICGtesting.com
Printed in the USA
BVHW051135281122
652924BV00009B/174